Pussley Seasons and the Nine Lives Five

A fantasy set in a feline world that finds Pussley and her band on their rise to fame and success.

Thomas Andrew

The Reading Glass Books
1-888-420-3050
www.readingglassbooks.com
fulfillment@readingglassbooks.com

Acknowledgment

This is an acknowledgment to three savvy women, who all happen to be from Long Island, New York. Sandi, Kerry, and Marilyn all live in different parts of this country now, yet they have all become an integral part of my storytelling. I don't know what was going on up there, but I will say, it must have been "something in the water."

I want to thank Sandi and Kerry for always being there to allow me to bounce ideas off them. They always respond with honesty and directness, interspersed with splashes of laughter. For that, I'm forever in their debt.

Thanks also to my editor, Marilyn, who I believe is great at what she does. A professional for her tireless multiple perusals of the stories, to remove grammatical or contextual errors. She's always quick to suggest a word or phrase that reels me back in with her hook of reality and logic. For her invaluable input, anecdotes, and humor, I am forever grateful.

So once again, a wonderful shout-out to all these smart, sassy, and intelligent women of Long Island!

Table of Contents

Chapter 1

It was at practice in the garage of Tinkles' owner that Mushkins decided she was not going to sing any longer. Her litter of kittens would be coming soon, and a garage band was no place for wee ones. The band was devastated! Their whole sound had been created around Mushkins' voice!

Practice ended, and everyone had their cream and fish sandwiches. Looking defeated, Yanx called Maxipuss and told him the news. Max, always landing on his feet, told Yanx, "It's only a minor setback. I'll peruse *The Daily Meow* and see if something jumps out at me." He was confident that he would find them a real purrer by next Saturday's rehearsal. After all, the treats had to keep coming.

Tinkles had just finished writing another song and really needed to hear a cat that could groove out front, pushing the band to become better, tighter, and more seasoned.

On Friday afternoon, Max had lined up several felines to audition. As the band was warming up, the first wailer came through the kitty door.

Petunia always wanted to be a singer. She looked fantastic and had a beautiful bushy tail, but when she started to sing it sounded like somebody had stepped on it.

Max said, "Thank you very much for coming, and next!"

Then in walked Kitty Purrin. Kitty was given the lyrics to "Walkin' the Edge," a classic number that Tinkles wrote several years earlier, which had become a favorite of the cool cats in Purrville. But when her cue came up to begin singing, she missed it!

Tinkles said, "That's okay, let's start it again."

And when it started, Kitty missed it again!

"So," Tinkles asked her, "Are you nervous?"

She didn't say anything, so Tinkles asked once again, "Are you nervous, Kitty?"

Kitty turned around and said, "Huh?"

That's when the band realized that Kitty couldn't hear very well. This sweet feline was born deaf in one ear, and as much as the band wanted her to do well, Max stepped in and said, "You've got a lot of heart, kid, but we kind of need you to be able to hear well. So, we're going to pass on you, Kitty. Thank you for coming."

Just when it looked like it was going to be a long afternoon, in walked a plain Jane kind of kitty cat, named Pussley Seasons. When she scanned the room, she noticed Kiddy Rock, the bassist who had played for her one evening at a talent show downtown. Then Kiddy Rock said, "Hey, I remember you! You were that singer with an amazing voice!"

Max perked up and said, "Well, okay, let's give it a go!"

The first four bars of "Walkin' the Edge" began, and Pussley came in right on cue. As she was singing, the band looked at each other, smiling. Why, she was singing better than Mushkins! She hit some notes that weren't even in the song! That had Tinkles grinning like the Cheshire Cat. When the song ended, there was complete silence. Max, seeing that that was his moment, asked Pussley if she'd like to be the new singer. Pussley let out a meow! That had everyone laughing and smiling.

"You're in, kid," said Max, "Tinkles, show her the setlist."

Max was tickled with Tinkles and their new discovery and brought several cans of sardines back for the band to enjoy.

Chapter 2

Saturday's rehearsal was never better. Pussley not only filled Mushkins' shoes, but she brought a half dozen of her own songs with her that were just as catchy. You could say they were the cat's meow!

Their next show was still two weeks away, and finalizing all the songs they had now was an exciting challenge, as it would bring them one step closer to being a real, professional rock band. Their dream was to play in large venues and arenas, and it seemed that reality was always just out of reach. Still, they were willing to hold on to it, gathering around at the end of rehearsals and talking about what it would be like to play in front of 10,000 cats, all purring and grooving to the music they were making. Max came in and told the band that at their next show, two talent scouts would be there from Kitty Corner Records, and that a good show may land them the record deal of their lives! All nine of them! From that moment on, it was all they could think about. They began practicing three times a week to be completely comfortable with all the new material. Things were going great, the band was playing well, and Pussley was singing wonderfully. Max was happy. The show was in three nights, and the band was ready, anticipating a stellar performance.

With one more evening of practice before the show, Pussley went by the vet's office to get some medicine for her brother Kit, who was home in bed with a very bad cold. When she walked in, there were a dozen cats all in different stages of the same cold her brother had. As she sat there waiting to see the vet, she noticed her throat was starting to feel a little scratchy. There wasn't cause for alarm, she was just aware of that feeling you get when you know something's coming on. *I'm not sure how this will go*, she thought. She received Kit's medicine and left.

Walking in the kitty door, she asked Tinkles if there was any hot tea that she could have. Tinkles said, "It's nice that you want to have the best voice possible for tomorrow night's show."

Pussley said, "Yes ... the very best!" But she could feel her throat growing more painful by the minute. *Oh meow! Why couldn't this happen two nights from now?* she thought.

The next morning, Pussley woke up with a high fever and could barely make it out of bed. Luckily, her brother Kit was getting better and, although he was moving slowly, he said he would help. Kit called Max and told him what was happening with Pussley.

Max swallowed hard and thought, *I am surely going to use up one of my lives over this one. What am I going to tell the band?* Max, always a straight shooter, called for a meeting that afternoon.

"Cool cats," Max began, "I've got some bad news." You could hear a pin drop.

Almost in unison, the band said, "What kind of bad news?"

"Pussley has come down with a high fever and is in bed. She can't even walk on all fours. She's struggling. Her brother Kit just called me and said she can't even talk."

The room was silent. Sum Tin said, "I hope she gets better quickly!"

"Not fast enough, kids," Max said. "We're going to have to cancel the show this evening, and hopefully we'll get another shot when the labels can come out and hear us."

Tinkles and Kiddy Rock said, "It's okay. We'll get another shot."

Catzenjammer said, "I'm going home and changing my strings again. See you at the next rehearsal."

Yanx just walked off, not saying a word. The meeting ended as fast as it started. Even though the wind was out of their sails for now, Max was determined to make heavy cream out of this. Since there would be no replacement to sing for Pussley, he wondered if there was another door he just couldn't see yet.

Chapter 3

Max scoured the Daily Meow, and looking in the back, he saw a little article that read:

> "A Battle of the Bands is Coming to Purrville. First prize is five whole cases of Furry's Lip-Smacking Chicken Treats. Also, the winning band will get to open for Kinfur at the Cats and Dogs Festival with 15,000 in attendance! To participate in the musical festivities, sign-ups end this Friday down at Club Pounce."

Max flipped to the front page … *That's tomorrow!*

Max made his way downtown and met with the club owner, Pudee Wood, an ex-army lion who had served two tours in Kathmandu. Pudee was now a big fan of promoting original music.

"Cutting it kind of close, aren't you there, Max?" Pudee quipped.

"I don't know, I still have all my fur!" Max shot back, smiling.

"Indeed!" said Pudee, and the two became friends right there.

Pudee asked Max, "What's the name of the band?"

Max, thinking fast, changed the name from Tinkle Time to Pussley Seasons and the Nine Lives Five.

"That's a catchy name," said Pudee.

"I just thought of it," said Max. "It was Tinkle Time, but every time I heard it, I was looking for a litter box!" They both meowed and laughed!

Max thanked Pudee for his military service, they both said their goodbyes, and Pudee wished him good luck.

Max, while on his way back, was trying to think of how he was going to tell Tinkles the name of the band had been changed. Max called Pussley first to cheer her up with the news that another possible opportunity for stardom was coming their way. Pussley growled with delight! She couldn't wait to get better. By the time the next rehearsal came around, the mood was somewhat somber. Max, looking over the room, saw everyone but Pussley in there ... and the band noticed it too.

Tinkles, not wanting to play with a gray cloud hanging over them, started playing a new tune for the band to listen to. It was a very pretty ballad he'd been working on, which changed the mood in the room. With that happier change, in walked Pussley. Upon seeing them, she felt terrible that the timing wasn't what it should have been, but the band rallied around her and had a big group hug, with Tinkles saying, "Don't worry about it, honey, something will come along."

Max, sitting in his chair reading the paper, pulled it down away from his face while smiling, and said, "Kids, I've got good news, and I've got real good news!"

They all stopped what they were doing and were all ears. Max told them he had signed them up for the upcoming "Battle of the Bands" down at Club Pounce next week, and that was exciting enough!

But of course, Yanx, the drummer, asked, "So, what's the real good news, Maxi?"

Max stated, "That if you take first place, you're going to be opening for Kinfur at The Cats and Dogs Festival, where there will be over 15,000 cool cats in the audience! They were stunned! Shocked! Then the awe set in. Their dreams were so close!

"And along with that," Max added, "We will have five whole cases of those chicken treats you guys love!" The band started meowing!

Chapter 4

"There is one thing," Max mentioned. "I had to change the name of the band."

Looking at Tinkles as he said it, they were all wondering out loud, "What did you change it to?"

"Well, when I told the club owner our original name, he said it reminded him of having to go to the cat box."

Catzenjammer laughed, shaking his head. Sum Tin Wong giggled. Kiddy Rock put his head down, shaking it back and forth. Tinkles, surprised, said, "I didn't know everyone felt that way about it."

"We didn't want to offend you. After all, you're writing such good songs," said Catzenjammer.

"We do love your music!" the band said together.

Upon hearing that, he looked at everyone and said, "Ahh, what's in a name anyway?"

So then Tinkles turned around, looked at Max, and said, "So, what's our new moniker, Boss?"

"You cats are now called Pussley Seasons and the Nine Lives Five."

There was a momentary pause, with Tinkles being the first to say, "I like it!"

Pussley, too, was delighted! She let out a meow and bounced over to hug Max. The band was happy they had a new name with new music to work up. They had a Battle of the Bands to prepare for, and hopefully, they would take the first-place prize for a chance to get closer to living their dreams.

Later that day …

The piano begins with a beautiful ballad that Tinkles has been working on. Drums and bass lay down the bottom, and Catzenjammer gives them a sweet intro, then plays the rhythm an octave higher. Pussley wants to sing something but has no lyrics yet. The song came to a halt, but everyone was feeling the magic taking place. This song needed the best lyrics, STAT! Pussley offered the fact that her brother Kit writes poems and songs for himself. She said, "I've seen some of them, and they're quite lovely."

Tinkles told Pussley to call him and get Kit down here. "We have a storm brewing."

Pussley asked her brother to bring all of his poems and songs with him. She told him that they needed something really special. Kit told her he had just finished something several days earlier that he liked.

"How soon can you make it here?" Pussley asked.

"I'll be there in a frisky minute," Kit replied.

While everyone was taking a break, enjoying some chicken treats, Kit glided in. Tinkles had a table already set up for him to spread his life out on. Every emotion Kit ever felt was on those papers. Pussley came over and looked at the newest one, picked it up, and started walking around the room with it in her paw. She was making moving gestures, creating a melody in her head. After a few minutes, she let out a meow. "I've got something I would like to try," she said.

Everyone took their places, and the song began. It created such a good vibe. Pussley started singing and was feeling it so well that Max came out of the office and stood there listening. The story was so moving that some of them even had tears. When she had finished, the room was silent.

Max walked into the circle of musicians, started clapping, and said, "That is the most beautiful song I have ever heard." Then he said, "Friends, I believe we have a hit on our paws. Studio tomorrow at 10:00 a.m., everyone be there."

Max went to make the phone calls. Tinkles said, "Let's go over this a few more times, my paws are tingling!"

With each run through, it seemed to get even better. They were making the song theirs. They now had the right lyrics, the right singer, the right musicians, and they were all in the same room, creating something beautiful. This was lightning in a bottle!

They recorded "Because of Your Fur" the next morning. They poured their hearts into it and produced what was to be their single in only two takes! It would take a little while to edit and complete the master, but it was worth the wait. The excitement of the band pulling together and giving it their all solidified their friendship for years to come.

The eve of the battle had arrived. Yanx had new skins on his set; Kiddy and Catzenjammer had the best strings on their instruments; Tinkles' keyboard sounded like an orchestra; and Pussley's voice was in fine form with Sum Tin harmonizing beautifully backstage.

Chapter 5

The Battle of the Bands rules were: You get to play two original songs, and at the end of the last band's performance, Mr. Pudee Wood would place his paw over the band and listen for the audience's approval. The band with the most meows and caterwauling would take first prize. There were six bands on the roster for the evening, and the club was packed! Band after band came out and played their two originals. Some were pretty good, others sounded like the same stuff that was being played in garages all across Purrville, but the fifth band to go on, Cats Have Staff, was very good. It was evident that The Nine Lives Five had much respect for them. As far as the band was concerned, they were the competition.

After they finished, the stagehands began setting up for Pussley's band. Their friends and fans were eager to hear them play. Waiting backstage, they could hear some musicians from the other bands talking about how good Cats Have Staff were and that they would probably win it. But that didn't bother them. They all felt they were holding onto a special box that, when opened, would spread their musical magic around the room, and audiences would come to feel the love as much as they did.

Now the room was quiet, and it quickly darkened! Then three … two … one … the lights suddenly popped, and they were on!

They opened with "Walkin' the Edge," a crowd favorite which was loved by the locals, and then came "Because of Your Fur." Looking into the crowd, Pussley noticed that all eyes were on her. They were mesmerized by her, and yes, some tears could be seen. When they finished, the crowd applauded enthusiastically, leaving them feeling they may have a very possible win.

While all the bands were backstage cleaning up and getting ready to come back out front, a dozen of the notorious City Bobcats, a biker club, rolled in. They spread out in positions throughout the room, telling all the cool cats in the audience that Cats Have Staff would be the winners this evening … "or else."

The bands came out and assembled on stage while the audience was told to quiet down so the applause could be measured. The first band had Pudee's paw over them, and the response was lackluster. The second band went on, and there was a smattering of applause. The third and fourth bands received some cheering and loud clapping. Pussley's band went on, and there was a fairly good response, though Pussley felt that they were holding back. Then, Cats Have Staff were out front and center. When Pudee's paw went over the band, the room erupted in chaos with screams and meows that wouldn't stop! The club clearly had a winner.

The band packed it up and left. The ride back to the garage was very quiet, while they were trying to figure out what had gone wrong. Tinkles was the first to speak. "Please don't let this evening stay with you. You are all fine musicians, and I was as proud as a roaring lion up there tonight with you. And I hope that while we played, it brought you to another world."

With one after another admitting there was no better time than tonight when they were playing together, Tinkles continued, "Then let's keep that magic going. We have something very special here, and I would love to see where the fates are taking us."

Tinkles threw his paw up, and the band returned the gesture, all touching each other's paws. They were all in for a penny and in for a pound.

Chapter 6

Kit was asked by Tinkles and the band if he would like to be the one who writes their songs. Tinkles would provide the melodies; the band would work them up and perform them. Not only was Kit honored by the request, but it also fulfilled his lifelong dream of expressing himself about how he looked at things, and possibly finding out that many others felt the same way.

Despite the loss at the Battle of the Bands, the group was enjoying the new chemistry that was present, and rehearsals were eagerly looked forward to. In the several months of playing together, they had created many songs they thought could be album-worthy.

That Saturday the band members, like so many other cats, attended The Cats and Dogs Festival. The weather was perfect, the food and treats were delicious, and the music was inspiring. Yes, Cats Have Staff opened for Kinfur, but there seemed to be a tussle between the two bands as their prize-winning opening acts were leaving the stage. Cat egos can be so petty!

Tinkles was driving the band back in his van. He had turned on their favorite station, KPUR radio, and as one of their favorite songs was ending, the band was talking about the timing on one of their newer tunes. Just then, a new song came on the radio, with the DJ introducing it as, "taking the country by storm!" The band's name was Pussley Seasons and the Nine Lives Five! The song was climbing the charts! And there it was … "Because of Your Fur."

Their song was on the radio, being heard by tens of thousands! In between screams and meows, they all sang along with it, grinning from ear to ear.

Max called Tinkles on the phone. "Are you listening? We're climbing the charts! I've had three calls already this morning wondering what our tour schedule looks like, but I didn't even have one to give them!"

Max and Tinkles laughed hard. A tried-and-true lesson was learned that day. In life, there are days you will succeed and others where you will fail. Every day is a learning experience, and with wisdom and dignity, you can see the value of both.

Chapter 7

Max got a call from Kittie Corner Records, asking if the band he managed had any more songs. If so, they wanted to produce an album for the band and promote them nationally! At this moment in time, their song, "Because of Your Fur," was being played everywhere. If they were writing and creating music of this caliber, there may be many more hits to follow. Max expressed his interest and mentioned that he could arrange a meeting with them that afternoon to discuss the details, especially about how it would benefit the band. As a manager, Max looked out for his cats. They were his world, and he was more like a father figure, making sure that his teenage children didn't get swindled or do something silly or dangerous.

Growing up in the suburbs of the city, Max didn't have a father to look after him because his father met with a tragic accident when he was very young. His mother had to take on the roles of both mother and father. She really did the best that she could, having four kittens to raise by herself. Max and his three sisters were given as much love and wisdom as a tabby mom could give. Being around all those girl kitties, it was natural for him to be the protector, the White Knight, and being the only male from the litter, his destiny had been created for him.

This role as manager of the band was one that he fit into comfortably. Going to bat for his band, looking for the best deal possible, is what would give these kids a running start and a fighting chance for the happiness in life that they sought. Many times, the music business had taken musical hopefuls, recorded their talents, and left them behind, looking for the next best thing and leaving the artists with little to no treats whatsoever! But Maxipuss would never let something like that happen on his watch.

Max arrived at the Kitty Corner studio office and was asked to wait a few moments before the owner and founder of the label, Hymee the Himalayan, would be in. This gave him a chance to reflect and remember where this had all started.

Max knew from the beginning, when he met Tinkles playing in a small restaurant for treats, that the music was in him. His melodies were creative, moving, and easy to listen to. He could tell by watching the others in the room letting their food grow cold while they stopped to listen, that Tinkles had them in the palm of his paw. It was that very same evening that Max asked Tinkles if he had a manager.

Tinkles' reply was, "What's that?"

"That's me looking out for you, kid," Max said. "Stick with me, Tinkles. I'll put you in nicer venues to share your music with, you'll never go hungry, and you will always have a warm place to sleep at night."

Tinkles purred at the thought and said to Max, "That sounds perfect to me!"

Some time has gone by since those days. Max was now the proud manager of a wonderful group of musical young cats who were ready to take on the world, and these kids weren't your average day-to-day puddy tats. These cats were special and very talented. Now, with Pussley out front singing the songs, a whole new dynamic had been introduced … the last piece of the puzzle; the icing on the cake. They were now being asked to make an album!

The meeting went very well. Hymee and Max hit it off famously. The studio was just as excited as Max to get these talented youngsters in front of the studio mics and record these rising stars, getting them down on wax, as the saying goes. You must strike while the iron is hot. The saying is an oldie but a goodie, appropriate when it comes to seizing the moment, and the moment at hand belonged to Pussley and the band.

Tinkles and his crew had approximately seven songs that they thought were their best to put down on that album. All seven songs were filled with emotion, melodically beautiful, musically challenging, and in several cases … haunting. These songs, once heard, stayed with you. Pussley's interpretations of Tinkles' melodies were nothing short of genius. They were authentic, heartfelt, powerful, and very dynamic. The harmony supplied by Sum Tin had become a necessary vocal element, with all the makings for a band's musical legacy to last a lifetime. The Nine Lives Five players all came to the table with unique musical abilities, but what Max and the studio came to love most about them was their normalcy: their ability to laugh at themselves, with no egos and no agendas. They took the music seriously … as they knew they had to. Yet they were still just a clowder of multi-talented cats wanting to share their talents with the world.

Chapter 8

The band gave the recording session their all. Some even said it was the best they've ever played. Now it was up to the studio engineers to bring the magic to the vinyl and for the studio to spread the news to all cats, young and old, that there's a new cat in town, and her name is Pussley Seasons. With her band, The Nine Lives Five, these musicians of sheer talent were going to rock and roll everyone into the next dimension, creating music they can't wait to listen to and sing along with.

Max received word from Kinfur's manager, Philly Shnizlestix, asking if his band would like to open for Kinfur for the northeast part of the tour starting next week! Max told Philly that the date he wanted them for was a little too early. He was hoping that the album would have been done and ready for sale by now.

Philly told Max, "Hold on there, biker dude … we don't need them to have more hits than we do!" He said this, laughing. "And yes, I remember you back in the day, when you were with the City Bobcats."

"Oh, come on, Philly, that was a lifetime ago!"

"It's how I remember ya!" said Philly.

"Ancient history, Tabby One," Max said, using his old nickname for Philly.

"Oh, so you do remember?"

"With a last name like Shnizlesticks, you were hard to forget!"

Philly laughed.

"But let's just leave that back there," said Max. "Let me think this over, Philly. What's the last possible date that we could have, if we were to join you?"

"All right, now we're talking! I'll get back to you with an answer in an hour."

Max was excited for the band and was waiting patiently for the phone call from Philly. In the meantime, he called the studio and asked for a progress report, and they told Max the album would be ready by Friday to ship out. Max took a seat as the reality that this was happening surprised him. As mind-boggling as it was, it was also very welcome. A whole new chapter for the band was about to unfold, and it was well-deserved. They put the work in, the right talent finally had come together, and with the release of "Because of Your Fur," this feline nation would be ready for Pussley Seasons and the Nine Lives Five on their first tour!

Philly called and said, "Could we see you in two weeks?"

"Philly, that's perfect timing," said Max. "I'll go break the news to the band. You and I will work out the details."

"This is going to be a lot of fun, Max!"

"It has to be Philly, I want these kids to enjoy themselves in the best of ways."

"I understand, dude," said Philly.

Max called a meeting, and everyone thought it was going to be about the need for more rehearsal time, but Max said, "No, you're going to get plenty of that."

"How so?" asked Tinkles.

"Well, because you're going to open for Kinfur, on the northeastern part of their tour."

It hit everyone like a freight train!

Catzenjammer said, "Are you serious?"

Pussley asked Max, "Are we talking multiple cities?"

"Major, young lady, major! And it gets better!" said Max.

Kiddy Rock said, "How could you possibly top that, Max?"

Max started walking away and said in a low voice, "Because your album is coming out next week."

Yanx heard it, and he actually growled like the MGM lion!

Everyone was sitting around the table, looking at each other, not quite sure what to say. The depth of all this was breathtaking! Tinkles started laughing, then everyone slowly started laughing, then Max looked at everyone with tears in his eyes and said, "We've made it; we have arrived; we are somebodies."

The whole band had tears in their eyes. Max walked over to the table, opened his paws wide and said, "Come here, kids, give me a hug!" And it was the best hug they ever had! If your hearts are true and your passions are strong, perseverance will bring you to your dreams!

Chapter 9

The band hit Philadelphia that afternoon, and Max checked them into the hotel. Philly met Max in the lobby, and they touched paws. Philly greeted the band and thanked them for coming and joining Kinfur on this part of the tour.

Pussley said to Philly, "It is our pleasure, Mr. Shnizlestix."

"Well, I see you've been talking to Max. What else did he tell you?"

"That he's known you for years, and he was surprised that you both wound up being in the music business."

"That is wild, kids. Max and I go way back … but that's another story," said Philly, looking at Max. Oh, and please call me Philly. We've got the afternoon, so where's all your gear?"

"Kit drove behind us; it's all in the trailer."

"Great. I'll have my cats take it off the trailer and load it in. We're only two blocks away from the Canine Club East. For the past several years, we've started here, kicking off our northeastern part of the tour, and now I'm happy to say you cool cats are part of it!"

Smiling, the band walked around the lobby of the place, admiring its glamor and size. Max told Philly they'd be over there within the hour to set up for the sound check, but first, they were going to get settled in their rooms.

As the elevator doors opened, there was Kinfur. Music was blaring, and they were throwing a Frisbee in the hallway, with half-eaten chicken treats littering the floor. Smells of a dirty cat box filled the air. Their drummer was even riding a motor scooter up and down the hallway!

The singer, Tab the Hunter, seeing the stunned looks on their faces said, "Don't worry, we have the whole floor!"

Almost in unison, they all faked a smile as they walked past the mini circus to get to their rooms. Max hadn't said a thing. This wasn't anything he was used to, either. They were given four rooms down the hallway on the end with adjoining doors in between each room.

As soon as the door closed behind them, Tinkles said to Max, "What was that?!"

"That was five cats with no manager present!" Max replied.

Pussley said, "I'm glad you're with us, Max!"

"Like glue, cool cats, like glue …"

The venue was large and could seat 5,000. The stage was enormous! It was bigger than anything they'd ever played on. This was the kind of place they would go to see a concert, not give one. Half a dozen roadie cats were moving all the band's equipment in and placing it on the stage.

Catzenjammer was getting ready to hook up his rig when one of the work cats said, "Hold on there, Tabby boy. All you have to do is tell us where you're going to stand and play, and we will do all the setup for you. When you're on tour with Kinfur, you don't have to set anything up; we do it all."

The band looked at each other, shaking their heads and smiling. They liked this touring thing a whole lot. Each one picked a spot where they were going to be comfortable playing, then Philly came out from behind the backstage curtain and asked the band to come on back and meet the fellas in Kinfur. Philly introduced his band members to them, and Max introduced his members to theirs. Everyone was smiling and purring.

Max's band had knots in their tummies with the anticipation of knowing that they were going to be up there performing to a packed house in just three hours.

Pussley went up to Philly and said, "Mr. Shnizlesticks, I want to thank you. This has been a dream of mine for as far back as I can remember."

One by one, the rest of the band chimed in saying, "Mine too!"

Then Max stepped in, looked at everyone, and said, "Mine too."

Everyone laughed at that. Tab placed his paw on Pussley's back and walked her to the very front of the stage, away from everyone. Looking out over the thousands of seats, he said to her, "This is where you will find yourself. You will find your freedom here, and when the crowd roars after each song, you will know why you are here."

The band never sounded so good, and this was just the sound check. After the cats at the mixing board gave a paws-up on the sound, Pussley glanced over at the side of the stage, where Tab was standing, listening. He gave his own paws-up to her, letting her know it sounded good. The band congratulated each other for a successful check and were now smitten with the desire to play their very best for the famous Canine Club East's sold-out show.

They all had just enough time to get their baths, a little food, and to make it back as the opening act for their first American city show! They got to play for forty-five minutes, through all seven of the songs that were on their new album. The last song was "Because of Your Fur," which sent the crowd into a frenzy as they finished!

At that moment, Kinfur realized just how big the Nine Lives Five were going to be. In the fifteen minutes it took for the bands to change gear, Kinfur greeted Nine Lives backstage and congratulated them on a performance well-done! The band was on top of the world, with the crowd still roaring loudly!

Kiddy Rock thought that the crowd was cheering for Kinfur taking their places on stage, but the curtain was still closed. That applause was for their band! When the curtain opened up and Kinfur appeared, Tab asked the audience, "What did you think of Pussley Seasons and the Nine Lives Five?"

The room exploded with cheering, whistling, roaring, and growling. Everything those cats and dogs could muster. Thankfully, Tab didn't have a big ego, so he said, "They're going to be with us for the next few months on our tour, so get your tickets and come see us all again."

He grabbed his mic and took his position. He looked to the right, looked to the left, dropped his paws, and the show was on!

Meanwhile, backstage, everyone was congratulating Pussley Seasons. They were telling her how beautifully she sang and how awesome the musicians were. They added that they couldn't wait to see them perform again. The band never had that kind of praise showered on them before, and they really didn't know quite how to take it. Seeing them uncomfortable, Max stepped in and took the questions and the praise for the band, giving them some room to breathe.

Back at the hotel, they couldn't stop talking about the evening. And unbeknownst to everyone, Philly had called some journalists from some top magazines to be in the audience and write about what they thought. The next morning, Max picked up the newspaper and summarized the comments to them, "Kids, they're saying you're the best thing since heavy cream. Get this, they're also saying it's one of the best shows that they've ever seen there."

Then he quoted, "This new band, Pussley Seasons and the Nine Lives Five, are really something!"

"And listen to this … they're telling everyone our album is out and on sale."

Max added, "People are lining up outside on the sidewalks in front of the record stores, waiting for them to open so they can get their copies of 'Because of Your Fur'."

"Kit cats, the train is just leaving the station, so buckle your seatbelts, your song is climbing the charts, and I believe we're in for one heck of a ride."

Chapter 10

The next show, their second, was in two nights. It would be the weekend, and the show with them opening for Kinfur was already sold out. Philly called Max and asked if he would mind if he sent over his makeup and wardrobe team that Kinfur uses for all of their public appearances. Max thought about it and said he would like to see some drawings or pictures of what Philly's team had in mind.

"That's a great idea, Max!" Philly said. "I'll get right on it and send you a couple of my pros over there. How does 11:00 a.m. sound?"

Max said, "It works for me."

The band had just come back from breakfast when the knock on the door came right at 11:00. Max went to the door, said, "Come in," and in walked a very professional-looking pair. They were a tom clothier named Felix, but everyone knows him as PQ (Prides Quarterly), and a queen makeup artist named Cutie Patootie. Max touched their paws and said, "It's nice to meet both of you."

He was impressed immediately and asked if they brought the drawings for the new look. Cutie went first. She stood next to Max and opened her book on his hotel desk. Max let out a meow! Cutie Patootie had taken pictures of the band the other night while they were on stage performing at the Canine Club East. All were taken from the front row, and she had worked her magic to show the band as five cute and adorable Nine Lives Five players. Then she turned the page, and Max said, "Who is that?"

"That is Pussley Seasons, Max."

"Whaaat? This beautiful feline is Pussley?"

"Yes, and in less than an hour, I can have her looking like this at every show. PQ, come on over here, open your folder, and show Max what can be a reality for this band, two shows from now."

PQ opened his folder and Max let out a growl! He said, "They look so professional! They could go on like this at every show?"

"Yes, sir, this could be the way the whole cat kingdom would see Pussley Seasons and the Nine Lives Five."

"Okay, I'm sold!" said Max, shaking his head. "But I have to talk with the band first to get their take on things." Max then asked, "May I have the two colored drawings of the clothing and the photographs of their new look?"

"Sure, Max," said Cutie. "When you decide something, let me know as soon as possible."

Max grabbed the phone, started dialing while looking at them both, and said, "I'm on it!"

Max called the band from the hotel and asked them to meet him that evening for dinner at the Oceanside, a very posh eatery where celebrities are known to dine.

"Grab a cab," said Max. "I'll cover it when you get there."

Right now, this band was on cloud nine. Their first concert was a success; media coverage was positive; they were being well-received in town; and their new album was selling fast.

"Your album is flying out of the stores!" Max told them.

Their record label, Kitty Corner, was jumping on the walls, digging their claws in, they were so thrilled.

Max had the waiters put the tables together to look like they were having a board meeting. Max met them in a tailored suit that fit him perfectly.

Catzenjammer said, "Gee, Maxi, why can't we go on stage looking like that?"

Max replied, "If you cool cats want to look this classy, I will make that happen for you."

All the band except Yanx roared in agreement!

"Oh, that would be the cat's meow!" said Sum Tin.

Pussley said, "That would really be something, Max! But as queens, Sum Tin and I wouldn't look too good in all that!"

"I agree, Pussley," said Max. "That's why I thought you two would like this look" … and Max took a folder out of his briefcase, laying out all of the pictures on the table. All but Yanx gasped!

Pussley said, "Oh, Maxi, could we really look like that?"

"Every night, sweeties," said Max.

Sum Tin purred loudly and Pussley wept.

"Max, you are so making my dreams come true. Words will never describe how I feel about your kindness and how you care for us."

"Awww … go on," Max said.

Yanx got up and walked away toward the restroom without saying a word.

Max looked back and told the band. "Order anything that you want. I'll be back in a few minutes."

Max walked in behind Yanx and sat down in the restroom attendant's chair. He spoke first. "Yanx buddy, how are you feeling about all of this?"

"Max, I love what you're trying to do for us. I really do. But there's no way I can see myself wearing that monkey suit while playing drums!"

Max laughed! He thought about it for a minute and suggested to Yanx, "What if I were to make you a suit without the sleeves for all fours and then make you a beautiful headband from the material matching the shirts! You would look completely different from everyone but still be recognized as the drummer in the band and the coolest cat up there!"

"Now you're purring and making bread, Maxi! I'm in!"

Max told Yanx, "Don't tell anyone about your new clothing choice. We'll surprise them at the third show."

"I love that idea, Max!"

Chapter 11

That night at dinner, the band got tighter and closer than they had ever been. It felt like a real family. Toward the end of their night, photographers had caught word of them being in the restaurant. Upon their arrival, they circled the table, taking pictures, walking all around the band with flashes going off. They were requesting poses and asking questions, while many of the patrons were asking, "Who are they?"

The waiters went around to the tables answering, "That is the new band that sings the song 'Because of Your Fur'," and with that, patrons were scrambling to get their autographs and to have pictures taken with them.

There was so much laughter, and everyone was having such a good time, that no one wanted it to end.

When they were finishing, Max said, "Everybody, come stand close behind me for a photo"—and bam!—there they were on the front page of the morning paper!

The photo showed Pussley Seasons and the Nine Lives Five out on the town with Max, smiling from ear to ear.

The first thing Max did that next morning was call Cutie, saying, "Bring your tailor, it's a go!"

Then Max called Hymee and let him know about the direction they were taking toward their stage presence.

Hymee said to Max, "Well done, Maxipuss. They will make great ambassadors for the label. Send all the bills to us, we've got you covered!"

Max and Hymee chuckled out loud with Max saying, "Good deal, Hymee!"

The lights were down, the band was taking their places for a packed house, and it was pretty quiet. You could feel the anticipation in the air. The stagehand who was standing off to the side asked, "Is everyone ready?"

They all said, "Yes." The countdown began.

Three … two … one … lights up! This room full of cats is going wild! The Nine Lives Five begin their set. Everyone is hitting on all cylinders; the piano is sweet in tone; the guitar is rocking the chords; the bass and drums have got the bottom end and are sounding like a freight train. Pussley steps out front and begins the song "Walkin' the Edge."

"Walkin' the Edge"

I don't know why
When I'm up here so high
There's no fear in my step
No fear of the ledge
I still have my lives
Haven't used any yet
I'm as cool as they come
I'm walkin' the edge

As she's singing, she looks out into the first five rows, sees a sea of cats singing with her, and realizes she has an audience. Cat paws wave in the air as she looks their way. She looks back at the band, and each one of them is looking at her, smiling. They all have her back. It's one of the best feelings she could ever feel as an entertainer. The transition from local club to major cities has been smoother than she ever anticipated. Her singing is stronger, more focused. With every note that leaves her, the energy is amazing, and she understands why Tab said, "You will know why you are here."

And yes, now she does. The set ended flawlessly with "Because of Your Fur," the recent hit from their debut album. As they all bowed, the roar of the crowd was deafening. Pussley reminds the audience to follow them on *Purrfect*. Then they all waved goodbye as they left the stage, smiling.

Backstage, everyone is talking about the energy that they were feeling on the stage from the crowd and from their own sound.

Sum Tin said, "Well, that was addictive!"

They all looked at her, but didn't need to acknowledge the obvious. Indeed, it was!

Tab came over, congratulated everyone, and thanked them for getting the crowd so crazy with excitement. Then he looked right into Pussley's eyes and said, "You're singing better and better with each show."

She replied, "Thank you, Tab, and go knock them out!"

Tab smiled and walked out front. Kinfur was still playing when the Nine Lives Five was looking to get a late dinner. Max asked the limo driver to take them to a quiet, out-of-the-way restaurant where they could relax, wind down, and eat in peace. They sat down at the table looking normal, perusing the menu like so many times before, but this time they didn't have to scrape change together, as their manager Max had this covered under expenses. Truth be told, he was enjoying himself immensely, not having to worry about getting paid ever again. He took in a deep breath and let it out slowly with the low hum of a gentle purr.

One queen cat who was across the way, sipping her cream, noticed Pussley and decided to come over, introducing herself as Felinia. Apologizing for the interruption, she spoke to Pussley, saying, "I remember you from Purrville."

"I remember you, too. How have you been?" Pussley asked.

Felinia replied, "I've been fine. I caught a bad cold for a little while, but I'm back and ready to move forward. Do you still sing?"

"Yes, more now than ever!" said Pussley.

The whole table laughed, and Felinia wasn't quite sure what to make of that.

"What brings you to Baltimore, Pussley?"

"We're on tour. We're opening for Kinfur."

"No way!" Then she got it!

"Way, Felinia. We started with them a week ago and will be with them for the rest of the tour in the Northern cities. The big one is coming up in several weeks ... that'll be New York City, at Mitzi's."

"Pussley, you are on your way to the top! I'm so very happy for you. May I ask who's helping to get things for you while you're on tour? I know how hard it can be to need to get something, but not have the time to do it."

"Well, there is that," Pussley said.

"And your manager is not going to be able to do that kind of thing for you. He has his own business issues to deal with. You can let him know I could be the band's runner, saving time for everyone."

Tinkles said, "That would be very useful to us."

Kiddy Rock said, "I could use something here today! I need a couple of sets of strings for my bass."

Tinkles went ahead and gave her the treats to go get them, and she was off.

Max came in moments later after filling out some permits and said he had to run right back out. Pussley stopped him for a moment and said, "Max, seeing that you are so busy, I've met an old friend that I've known from my Purrville days who can help us out. She would like to be our runner for the things that come up in everyday life that we will need, and you're not always going to be available for us, Maxi."

"You've got a point there, kid. Let me run it by the label."

"Thank you, Max, you're the best," said Pussley.

Everyone was cleaning and polishing their instruments when Max's phone rang. It was PQ, the tailor. He'd be up in about twenty minutes, and he had a small entourage with him. Max stood there looking around, just taking it all in and thinking how fast your lives can change for the better, and more often than not, it's because of talent.

Max told the band that PQ and his group would be up shortly. "They'll take each of you one at a time back into a room for a fitting and measurements."

Catzenjammer said, "Max, you really know how to get things done fast."

"I only want the best for you kids."

"And we love you for that!" Tinkles shouted, and the band shouted back, "Truth!"

PQ arrived with two finely dressed toms, eager to start taking measurements. Sum Tin and Pussley went first while the band cats continued to polish their instruments. Felinia came back with Kiddy Rock's strings and as she turned to leave Kiddy said, "Felinia, you don't have to leave so quickly. You're more than welcome to hang here with us."

"That's very kind of you. I think that would be fun!"

As far as the band was concerned, she had just become a part of their entourage.

Kit was in one of the other rooms writing songs. He and Tinkles were going back and forth, trying new things, playing with melodies, and doing what musical cool cats do. About the time PQ was done with the two queens, Cutie Patootie knocked on the door. Pussley opened it in one of her new outfits.

"It looks like I'm right on time," said Cutie. "Pussley, I'm going to make you up like the picture that Max showed you, then we'll take a few more pictures. You too, Sum Tin. Today's your day also!" she was meowing and laughing.

Spirits were high in those rooms that day. The band was getting a wonderful transformation in the way they would look.

PQ came up to Yanx, whispering in his ear, "You're going last, big fella. Max let us know just what you're looking for."

Again, with the making bread motions, "I'm all legs, and feeling the love," Yanx joked, smiling.

Chapter 12

The band is waking up, realizing that they're playing Mitzi's Water Gardens tonight with Kinfur in New York City. This will probably be one of the most important shows they will play for the rest of the year! Musicians, celebrities, label CEOs, industry giants, and anybody who is anyone will most likely be there.

After tonight's show, Tinkles is going to introduce two more songs for the band that he, Kiddy, and Catz have worked on for the past week, and they are very excited about them. With the seven songs from the album and three others that the band already knows, this gives them ten quality numbers for a solid opening set that everyone seems to be digging. Tinkles even told the band that he had seen Tab off to the side of the stage at their last show, singing the lyrics along with Pussley to "Because of Your Fur."

"Because of Your Fur"

How many more lives will you take from me?
Now that you've broken my heart
Kitten, please set me free
And when you did, my life was a blur
My balance thrown off all because of your fur
I no longer had refuge, for my nails to explore

43

My head to lay sleeping, dreaming kittens and more
The days are so long, never finding a cure
Love abandons me now because of your fur
The loss of your fur, I will tell you, I'm sure
Leaves no smile, just tears with no purr
As all cats' lives matter, mine leaves me in tatters
With memories of true love so pure
I remember the day, as you strutted my way
I gave you my cream and my treats right away
But now you've taken from me my desire to play
My last lives are empty for sure
This alley feels cold and has lost its allure
And it's because of you
Because of your fur

"The song is number three and still climbing!" Kiddy tells Pussley as Cutie is applying her makeup.

PQ, on the other side of the room, is laying out the band's outfits.

As Max scans the room, he knows there's not another band out there that looks as sharp as his cats do. Max thinks to himself, *This is what it feels like to have a winning team! Ascending to the top, all go and no stop.*

Sum Tin and Pussley work on a new harmony that Sum Tin is hearing in her head while Cutie is applying their makeup. It causes Tinkles to walk over and add his take on it, also. Everyone stops what they are doing because at this moment, these three are sounding like angels. This dynamic had never been heard before! After their singing came to an end, everyone in the room began laughing joyously!

They knew, for the second time, that they'd discovered lightning in a bottle! So, from this night forward, all of their songs and the next bunch of tunes that would be written— except for Pussley's hit song— would also be sung by these three singing in harmony.

Tonight is the night to wow them all, to show the world they have arrived, and to leave them wanting more.

Backstage, Kinfur comes up to Pussley and the band. Philly is leading the way. He and Max touch paws. Philly tells everyone that he and Kinfur are thankful to Max and everyone here for making this leg of the tour such a success, and that they have an announcement to make at the after-party that will turn everyone into Cheshire cats.

Chapter 13

The limousine ride to the after-party was quiet. Everybody expended every ounce of energy they had to give their best performance ever! Kinfur played their hearts out and got two standing ovations. Tab, the gentle tom that he is, asked the massive audience what they thought of Pussley Seasons and the Nine Lives Five. The applause was deafening.

The audience's appreciation was currently over the top, and their rise to stardom was assured.

Max, in the passenger seat, turned around and asked the band how they were feeling.

Yanx spoke first and said, "I feel like I just ran a marathon!"

Tinkles laughingly said, "I think all of my paws are numb!"

Kiddy said jokingly, "What a dive, I thought we were uptown?"

Everyone burst out laughing!

Catz said, "That was the best performance I have ever given!"

Max again said, "Queens, Tinkles, your vocals are nothing short of stunning, angelic, and yes … moving. I believe this band will be number one on the charts next month!"

Kit spoke, "It all seems so surreal. Just a little while back, I was writing poems on scrap paper; now I'm going to an after-party with one of the hottest bands in the country. Someone pull my tail!"

Again, the limo erupted with laughter. The limo stopped out in front of the Fritz. Philly was there to personally open the doors for the band and … boy, he could really work a crowd. One by one, as they exited the limo, photographers were calling them out by name, shouting, "Hey, Pussley! Look this way" or "Yo, Yanx, can I get a smile?" or "Tinkles, was this the best time you've had in New York?"

The band could not believe their popularity! Young, cool cats wanting autographs, fans wanting pictures with the band, even two musical youngsters had brought their guitars for Catzenjammer to sign. A regular feline circus! Everyone followed Philly, with Max looking back to make sure the whole band was moving forward into the banquet hall.

Pretty Little Felines was already on stage playing their version of Kinfur's "It's A Purrfect Night" as they entered. Tab came up to Pussley and asked her if she'd like to meet a few of his friends.

"As long as it doesn't take me away too long," she said. "I know Max would have a kitten!"

The band was seated at a big round table, and Max was taking his head count when he asked, "Where's Pussley?"

Sum Tin said, "Tab the Hunter wanted to show Pussley off to some of his friends and to take advantage of the photo ops."

Tinkles said out loud, "The press will have an absolute field day with that, suggesting all the kittens to come and the seedier, dirtier litter."

This caused Max's ears to perk up and tell the band, "Hipsters, I'm going to go find Philly, please stay here."

Calico waiters with trays of champagne and treats filled the empty spaces between the tables. The laughter, the chatter, the music … it was feline sensory overload! And it was all because of Kinfur and The Nine Lives Five playing together in one of the best shows that Mitzi's had ever seen.

Max was walking back to the table with Pussley when Philly got up on stage. He was speaking into the mic, asking for everyone to calm down for a moment because he had some exciting news to share with them. As the room quieted, he spoke and said, "The message I just received from Kitty Corner Records is, first of all, to thank Maxipuss Maxwell, the manager of The Nine Lives Five, for helping to create this wonderful new look for this amazing band."

The room erupted in applause, with meows, growls, and even screeches heard throughout the room. Philly asked Max to stand and take a bow. For the first time, the band saw Max blush, but they admired his spirit. While they clapped their paws all the louder Philly put his paws in the air to calm everyone down and said, "The second thing I would like to say, on behalf of myself and the band Kinfur, is that we would like to invite Pussley Seasons and the Nine Lives Five to continue performing with us for the remainder of the tour, which includes Europe!"

And with that, Max's and the band members' mouths dropped open.

Max turned around, looked at the band, and asked, "What do you think of that, cool cats?"

Pussley started crying. Tinkles came over and put his paws around her and said in her ear, "Your talent has brought us here."

Then she looked up at Tinkles and cried all the more. But indeed, they were the happiest of tears.

The rest of the band looked up at Philly and put their paws in the air. The excitement couldn't be topped, or so they thought. Philly asked for quiet once again and began to speak, "But I saved the best for last. Max, you haven't heard this yet. The label was going to tell you this in the morning, but as your friend, I would like to tell you now." There was silence as all eyes were upon him, patiently waiting for the words. "While the band was performing at Mitzi's, the ballad "Because of Your Fur" hit number one on the Feline Nations Top 100 Rock Chart! Congratulations, Max, and to all you fine musicians and singers who make up Pussley Seasons and the Nine Lives Five!"

More amazing applause. The band was numb. Max's head was somewhere on cloud nine. The band got up from the table with Max, and all of them gave a great big group hug. Max said, "I love you all, and I will continue to look after you for the rest of my days."

Tinkles shouted, "We wouldn't have it any other way, Maxi."

The band meowed loudly with happy tears running down their faces. It was a moment to be savored, like the finest tuna in oil from the coast of Spain. It was a well-deserved night to remember.

Chapter 14

The other day, Catzenjammer, while sitting down in the lobby reading a newspaper, overheard two young felines talking about a new song that they loved. He could hear from one of their phones that the song, "Walkin' the Edge," was now getting airplay! It wasn't with the new harmony that the band came up with; it was the original recording from the album. Still, it took him by surprise, and he raced up to the rooms to tell everybody.

Opening the door, he first saw Max. "Maxi," he said, "'Walkin' the Edge' is on the radio now!"

"That is fantastic, Catz! Let's go tell the others."

They knocked on the adjoining doors, got everyone together, and Max said, "Catz has something to tell all of you."

"'Walkin' the Edge' is now on the radio also!"

"Really?" squealed Sum Tin. "That is such a good song."

Kiddy said, "Yeah, that one really rocks!"

With that, Max asked, "Who's up for room service?"

Immediately, all of them meowed and said, "I am."

The band had three days to relax before the next show. Tab called Pussley to see if she would like to take in some of the sights that the city had to offer. He had already asked Maxi if it would be okay.

Max said to Pussley, "Please stay in touch with me."

"Sure thing, Max. Thank you." … and she was off!

Kiddy had asked Max if Felinia could start traveling with them, since she was always eager to please, being helpful to the band, and available when Max couldn't always be.

"I think that's a good idea, Kiddy. Because of your growing popularity, it's not the smartest move for you cats to go out gallivanting, looking for this and that. Go ahead and bring her in."

In his own mind Max thought, *Boy, I could use someone like that too!* And then he thought of his sister, the one he got along with better than anyone … Claire Dainty. Growing up, she always looked up to him and was always asking if there was anything he needed. She had such a good heart, and it would be nice to have family close by … so that afternoon, Max, too, made a call and brought in Claire as his Queen Friday.

Tinkles was working on a new song, a real rocker. With the melody, lyrics came to mind about playing music and touring. He asked Kit to write some lyrics around that idea. Kit smiled and said, "I think I can do that!" After hearing the progression of the song, he went into his writing sanctuary and put pencil to paper.

"Pushing Forward, Looking Back"

The road that's underneath us
Leaves another show done
While sitting on this tour bus
Dreams of cities that will come
We'll play for several hours
And give everything we've got
We'll go through all your favorites
And some new ones that are hot!

(Chorus) It's a cat's world,
Not a dog-eat-dog
They may have masters
But we have staff
Coming to your town
Putting all our love down
On to the next
With the bands' hardy laugh

We'd like your hearts to love us
And to sing our songs with us
To clap your paws
When given cause
And show appreciation
Gladdens our souls
Gives us highs without lows
And sparks our inspiration

Kit came back in twenty minutes to show Tinkles what he had.

Tinkles read it and was floored. "This is exactly what I was looking for, Kit! I think this will go nicely over the rhythm and melody." And so, Tinkles began working his magic ...

54

Chapter 15

Tab and Pussley were having a wonderful time out and about. Taking pictures, nibbling on local treats, signing an occasional autograph … this is what Pussley dreamed of doing while growing up, and now it was all coming true. She and Tab really were falling for each other. They both had an easy way about them, with much to like. As they were walking, Tab grabbed Pussley's paw and didn't want to let it go. He looked into her eyes and saw that she was happy to oblige. She was hoping that he would take the lead.

Back at the hotel, PQ came in with all the suits from the dry cleaners, but Yanx's headband wasn't among them. It seems that some frisky, sticky-pawed feline wanted a souvenir. All Yanx said was, "Ahh, the price of stardom."

"PQ, can you get me half a dozen of those, in a couple of different colors?"

"I've got you, Yanx," said PQ.

Kiddy was on the phone with Felinia, asking if she could make it to the Fritz here in New York, then stay for the rest of the tour as part of the small entourage that the band needed.

Over the phone, Kiddy could hear her meowing loudly. She told him, "I'll be there this evening."

"Looking forward to seeing you, dear," he said as they hung up.

Sum Tin was asked by Tinkles to add her wonderful harmony to his on the chorus of the new song.

Max was in Philly's room, going over the coming itinerary for the next three cities. All three shows were already sold out. This prompted Max to ask Philly who he could get in touch with to create the desired merchandise that everyone was asking for.

"Maxi, it just so happens that our graphic artist, Puddin Cup, who designs all our shirts and stuff, is here in New York. Let's give him a call and see if he can meet with us over here."

All Max could do was purr and say, "Outstanding!"

He then called the label to speak with Hymee and told them of the plans for merch. To this, Hymee replied, "As long as we get our percentage, Max, I say shoot for the stars. You're on a wonderful ride right now, and we couldn't be happier for you and your band. Go get 'em, tiger!"

Max hung up, being so grateful to the One responsible for making all this and everything possible.

Back in the hotel room, Catz and Kiddy were finishing up the guitars for Tinkles' new tune. From what they could hear, they had another hit on their paws and would no doubt start clawing the walls if Pussley didn't return soon to add her talents to the mix,

Max's sister, Claire Dainty, arrived at the hotel room and was invited in by Tinkles. Having met her once, he introduced her to the band members who were present. Then he called Max and told him of her arrival.

Max raced back down the hall and burst through the doorway, opening his paws wide for Claire to get a big, warm hug.

Although Max had a tough exterior, he sure was a softy inside, which made him all the more likable. Max, being the older brother, introduced her to everyone all over again, and they all just went along with it.

Max brought his sister a blanket for the couch and asked if she would like some tuna and chilled cream.

"You still remember what I like, Maxi!"

"Always will, sweetie," he said.

Max sat down next to her after she was finished and told her about the things he would need from her to keep the band going from city to city. Claire would keep things running smoothly and on time, while he would do his managerial duties. All phone calls would be handled by her, and arrangements that Philly needed to discuss would now be run past her first.

Max continued purring all the while he was speaking. When he finished, she told him it sounded like a lot of fun and asked him, "When can I start?"

"You just did!" said Max, laughing.

Chapter 16

"A Kitten's Lullaby"

I'll put you to bed, then kiss your sweet head
Wishing you many sweet dreams
Of baking fish pies, and kittens who fly
And to ride on the back of a queen
And if you should rise before I awake
Know that I've left you some cream and some cake
To calm your wee cries, you so often make

Fear not the quiet nor dark of the night
For soon the stars hide up above
And the sun it will shine
On kittens like you who are watched and protected
with love
So let Mama be at peace and in rest
For when I am up I do give you my best
But for now it's still dark
And meant for eyes closed
And to sleep till the dawn finds us blessed

This is a song that Catz wrote early on, remembering what
his mama had shared with him on those dark nights. He had
been playing with a working melody for over a decade, now

deciding to break it out and show Tinkles one evening in their hotel room. The melody on the guitar was pretty, but when Tinkles played the piano, the song came to life! Sum Tin and Pussley scrambled to learn the lyrics, while yelling at Catz for holding on to such a beautiful song.

"It never sounded like this!" he argued laughingly. The three-part harmony that Tinkles and the two queens brought to it solidified its destiny.

Catzenjammer, whose parents were owned by a German diplomat, had immigrated from Vienna to just outside of Purrville, and allowed the young tom to pursue his passions from an early age. Catz's grandfather was a concert-quality musician who traveled extensively during his career … something Catz always dreamed of doing. So, with a passion for the blues, he set out on his own musical journey, gleaning and learning from some of the best: Bebop Harrison, Franklin "Jonesy" Wallace, and Frightnin' Lightnin' Levi Rollins. These were some of the bluesiest cats ever to play, and Catz studied them all.

Copying all their licks and songs, along with his two years of musical theory studied at Deutsche Shule Für Feline Musik in Berlin, helped Catz to create his own style, with a lot of him thrown in as well, making him quite unique to listen to. A touring cool cat from a young age, Catz always had a chaperone sent with him by his papa, Liebe Katza. Catz was always a favorite at the clubs in Purrville.

Now, one evening some time ago, Tinkles was to play a show for a private party. Ten minutes before he was to go on, the guitarist's mate, who was about to have kittens, suddenly thought it necessary for him to be with her for their birth! The abrupt departure left Tinkles in a panic. He told Max what had just happened, which threw Max into fixer-mode. As he was thinking of what to do next, he was looking over the guests, deciding what he might have to say to them. But the fates were kind, and Max noticed a well-known guitarist among the many guests. So, Max approached him and asked him if he was interested in filling in for this emergency situation.

Catz replied, "I just gave a lesson to a friend several hours earlier, so I do have my rig with me. Would you like me to go get it?"

"I would love for you to get it, Catz," Max said, humbly and thankfully.

Max told Tinkles of their good fortune and explained that he had found a better guitarist to sit in. Tinkles was amazed at Max's expediency and at how he got things done so professionally.

Tinkles was calling out the chord changes on some of his original music, while Catz's playing was flawless and was highlighted with moments of brilliant soloing. This left the audience mesmerized, causing the party's owner to tip them well for the wonderful performance and for making his party such a success.

And thus began the relationship of Tinkles, Max, and Catz.

Chapter 17

The afternoon was coming to an end, but neither Tab nor Pussley wanted it to. The feeling of holding paws, of belonging to someone, was intoxicating for both of them. Everything that is seen when you're together is a point of view the whole world longs for, and gazing into each other's eyes, being in love, is the best therapy for any two felines in this crazy world we live in. The limo ride back to the hotel flew by, and in the elevator, it was decided that they wouldn't tell anyone of their new romance until further down the road.

Deciding to keep the secret, they both giggled like children finding cookies that Mom had hidden in the oven. They kissed, rubbed noses, and went back to their own hotel rooms, practically floating across the carpet, with each of them having to quiet down their own purring.

Max picked up another room for Claire and Felinia, who will now be with them full-time. They will be performing all the crazy running around that is needed for a budding band on the crest of stardom.

Their next show, in two days, is in the city of Hartford and is already sold out. The band is eager to play Catz's new song, "The Sun, My Son, Will Shine." If it is received as well as they believe it will be, they will be in the studio between shows. Max has also asked Hymee to send the recording team to Hartford to catch their performance of the new song live, before the studio date.

Hymee loves the idea and tells Max they'll be on the first flight out. Hymee called the film crew into his office and began relating to them how he would like nothing but the best for their new rising stars. He would like the entire show to be brought back here and mastered with the band all together on their first break.

"These young cats are going to be around for a while, and their success is ours also."

"You got it, H.H.!" said the crew chief.

Max also made the decision that he wasn't going to let the band know they were being recorded. He wanted everyone to see what Hartford was seeing. No veils, no masks, no acting … just them, having the time of their young lives.

Room service arrived in the morning, and while everyone was sitting at the large table, Max asked them all if they were enjoying the tour.

They could all be heard at the same time, "Yes, Maxi!"

"The best time ever, Max!"

"Our dream come true, Mr. Maxwell."

"Wonderful, kit cats! Play your hearts out tonight, because the fans really love you kids. What you're doing up there is bringing me mountains of joy!"

With that, Pussley started crying.

"Now, now, sweetie," said Max, "let's get down to business." Taking the covers off the trays, he said, "Let's fill our bellies with this breakfast deliciousness."

Smiling, they were eager to comply. That morning, they feasted on eggs cooked three different ways, sardines, tuna in oil, chicken livers, mackerel fillets, and honey biscuits with creamy butter! This was washed down with heavy cream, milk, or tuna-flavored sparkling water. Nothing but the best! Max had never seen the band eat so well, and he also enjoyed the fine meal.

Max told the band, "Don't forget, at 1:00 we have a sound check." Then he went back to his room to call Hymee to make sure the recording crew would be incognito.

Hymee assured Max, "They'll never know we're there."

The curtains opened and the band hit it running. In this crowd, not only were the cats screeching and wailing, but the dogs were also going into a frenzy! From the very first song, this Hartford crowd was showing their love, and the band was all smiles. Tab, watching from the side, couldn't help smiling with pride for his queen. She was charismatic, her voice was pitch-perfect, and her moves on stage were like those of a seasoned professional.

Several members of Kinfur mentioned that they liked the Nine Lives Five's sound better than their own and that it probably wouldn't take too long before they would be opening for them! Although they outwardly laughed, that possibility stayed with them. The set finished with Catz's song, "The Sun, My Son,

Will Shine." The harmonies were angelic, and the audience loved it, with tears easily seen in the eyes of those sitting in the well-lit first row.

The curtains closed, and Kinfur was gearing up to take their positions. Suddenly, their drummer, Cornwallis, tripped over some mic cords while walking to his set and sprained the wrist of his right paw! The band went into panic mode!

Tab came backstage and blurted out what had just happened, saying, "We're not going to be able to go on! Without the drums, we're sunk!"

That's when Yanx stepped in and said, "If you toms don't mind, it would be my honor to fill in for Cornwallis this evening. I mean, I do know all of his beats."

Everyone looked around, stunned!

Tab came up to Yanx and said, "You'd do that for us?"

"It would be my pleasure," he purred. "So, let's do this!" Yanx said as he now approached Cornwallis's drum set.

Tab looked back at Pussley and, with his eyes, seemed to say, "So kind."

Kinfur sounded wonderful! Yanx played brilliantly, and everyone backstage was smiling! The heavy cream flowed, and huge bowls of treats were on every table. Pats on the back with thank yous came from the band. Cornwallis came up to Yanx, asking him to show him some of those moves he did on his solo. Max and Philly both came back to congratulate everyone on their fine performances.

Philly came up and gave Yanx a special thank you with a hug and said, "You saved the evening. I won't forget this."

Yanx looked at Philly and, in front of everyone, said, "What were we talking about?"

Everyone present burst out laughing, meowing, and caterwauling! It was another epic evening!

Chapter 18

The press was having a field day talking up the new band.

Pussley Seasons and the Nine Lives Five are here in town, touring with Kinfur. Both lead singer lovebirds have been caught on camera here in downtown Hartford the day after the show. From the pictures, it looks like they are more than friends … holding paws, hugging and kissing, laughing up a storm … all the fun stuff couples do!

Although Tab was aware of the press presence, Pussley hadn't noticed anything. Her head was in the clouds. After all, it's not very often in one's life to feel this way about someone, and Tab didn't feel it necessary to crush their moment.

As Max was reading the morning paper, he opened it up to the entertainment section and there she was…Pussley. She was kissing Tab in front of a pizzeria.

The title read, "Ahh Romance! These Rockers Rocked the Town and Each Other for the Day."

Max didn't know what to think. He knows he's only their manager, but they're also kind of like his extended family. At least having a conversation with her may ease his mind.

Room service knocked on the door and entered with two large, wheeled trays. Max thought that while they were still in New York, they might as well try all the rave about the city's bagels with lox and cream cheese with a side of sushi! There was also an assortment of flavored heavy creams. The word was out … breakfast was served!

Kiddy Rock woke up and walked into the dining area with bedhead, smiling from ear to ear and saying, "I hope this never ends."

Max chimed in, "If you cool cats keep writing these hit tunes, this will be your new norm!"

"While making his bagel, Tinkles said, "Is this really our life now, Maxi? The best hotels, the best food, treats, limos, after-parties?"

Max said, "You're rising stars, kid. This is your shot. It's one in a million. You've all paid your dues and sacrificed much to make your dreams become a reality. And because all of you are so darn talented, when fate brought you together, your chemistry exploded: it became something else, something the world can't get enough of. So, let's ride this till the wheels fall off and enjoy this incredible gift."

"Indeed!" meowed Kiddy.

Felinia and Claire came to the dining area and helped themselves to a wonderful bagel and lox breakfast, leading Claire to say, "Maxi, how often does this happen?"

"Kitten, this is going to happen in every city we play in."

"My word! It's a wonder that band members aren't 500 lb. fluff balls rolling around the stage, trying to catch their breath!"

Max laughed hard at that one.

"You're killing me, Sis!" Max said.

After breakfast, Max told everyone they were going to get on the tour bus and head to Providence.

"Another sold-out show awaits you, cool cats."

Chapter 19

The night in Providence kicked off beautifully. The band was going through their numbers, and the applause after the songs was just deafening … growls, roars, and meows. Their songs were taking off, and at this time, they could do no wrong. Pussley's and Sum Tin's voices were getting better and better. Tinkles added his voice to the harmony and brought all of their songs to a new height. Tonight, the last song that they would leave the audience with would be "Because of Your Fur." It was loved by all and is now the number one song in America. As Pussley was singing it, she could see that practically the entire audience was singing with her. The song came to its end. As the band was getting ready to leave them to thundering applause and tears in their eyes, they bowed and walked off stage, only to hear the crowd calling them back, meowing, "One more song!"

"Don't go yet, play one more!"

Pussley looked at Tab backstage, and Tab said, smiling, "Well, don't keep them waiting. Go give them one more."

Coming back for their first encore ever, they gave the audience their newest number. It was Catz's song, "The Sun, My Son, Will Shine." While it was being sung, Catz walked over and shared a mic with Sum Tin, adding his voice, too, and the song got even better! No one in the band knew Catz could sing so well with his smooth German accent until this evening. As Tinkles was playing the beautiful melody, he realized how vocally strong this band now was. As they again bowed, thanking the feline and canine fans of Providence for giving them so much love, Pussley alone walked to the front of the stage and said, "Shortly, the band that you all have come to see, Kinfur, will be out here to rock your paws off. Show them your love, Providence!"

Tab was so thrilled with their introduction that he gave Pussley a big, long kiss and a tight hug that left her in a kitty coma, breathless.

The bus rolled into town and stopped in front of the nicest hotel. The band got out and was escorted up to their rooms. Onlookers murmured, "Who are they?" While hipster kitties knew exactly who they were, and their word traveled fast! By dinnertime, there were three hundred felines of all ages waiting to catch a glimpse of Pussley, the band, or Kinfur. It was turning into a circus, so hotel management had to call Philly to see if he could keep it down to a dull roar. The band had to stay up in their rooms because there wasn't enough security to ensure their safety with the crowds that had gathered. The lobby was now mobbed! Philly called Max up in his room and asked him if he had any ideas.

"Let's get Pussley down there and have her tell them that if they'll leave quietly, she will personally hand out some free tickets for tonight's show."

Max asked Philly, "How many do you have?"

"I've got twenty."

Max said, "I have ten. I'll have Pussley come down in thirty minutes."

"You're one slick cat, Max," said Philly. "I'll meet you down there."

Max told Pussley that she needed to be down in the lobby for a little while to hand out some tickets to the fans. She didn't know it was to appease the hotel management. She thought it was a photo op, so she was glad to do it. Sum Tin, Claire, and Felinia went with her. The elevator doors opened. Max led the way into the lobby, and right away fans were yelling for Pussley, crowding her, asking for her autograph, and Sum Tin was being asked also. Claire and Felinia stood there, amazed. They had never experienced anything like this. Cats of all ages were inside and out, trying to catch a glimpse of their new favorite singer. A camera crew even rolled in for the impromptu celebrity event. While all this was going on, Kinfur's bus had pulled up in front, and the band's players were getting out to be escorted to their rooms. The bassist and guitarist walked in practically unnoticed. Cornwallis was asked for his autograph, as was Tab. Tab, entering the lobby, removed his sunglasses and looked over at Pussley. Their eyes met, and she gave him the sweetest smile. He smiled in return, with a wave of his paw to her and went upstairs. After all, he was trying to be incognito.

With the tickets given away and the crowds dispersing, the four queens and Max headed back up to their rooms. They were unaware that Kinfur's bandmates were allowing jealousy to smolder with embers of green. They were saying things like, "They're just the opening band" or "They would be nothing without us!" and even, "Who do they think they are, stealing our fire?"

That's when Cornwallis chimed in and said, "Listen, you two hairballs … they're young, very talented, and have got some great songs selling out there right now, which is keeping these shows sold out. And don't forget that Yanx saved us the other night," said Tab. "So, cut them some slack and let them enjoy this."

They both walked away mumbling. Although that was the end of it, the seeds had been planted. Tab had no idea of the little kitty pity party that his bandmates were going to have.

Cornwallis, being a classy cat, never spoke a word of it again.

Chapter 20

The venue in Boston was open-air on a beautiful sunny day. Max was told by Philly, "There are fifty thousand cats and dogs in the stadium today, with more at the gates searching for tickets."

Max said, "If I'm thinking this is surreal and I'm backstage, I can't even imagine what the band is feeling looking out over that sea of felines and canines of every imaginable size and color!"

They were all there to see what the bands could do with the songs that they know, because that's the business of entertaining the masses. And that's exactly what Pussley and her band did, with flair and confidence, owning the stage and giving their all for a command performance to that sea of fifty thousand screaming fans.

The audience enthusiastically sang along with many of the band's songs. With each song's conclusion, the applause grew louder, creating a thunderous acclaim that fueled the band's onstage euphoria to unprecedented levels.

The depth of their voices singing in harmony and unity was beyond belief. With their set complete, they took their bows and walked off stage to deafening accolades. Still floating on air and in complete shock, they were numb from the continuous adrenaline rush.

They glided behind the curtain where Kinfur's members were taking their places, waiting for their introduction. Tab came up to Pussley, gave her a huge kiss, and told her, "That was the best performance I have ever heard your band play! Or any band for that matter. You truly were inspiring. You and your band are indeed destined for greatness." Then he disappeared onto the stage.

Max gathered his band together and enjoyed a group hug. It was so affirming and so congratulatory!

Max looked at every one of them and said, "I am so darn proud of each and every one of you." Max asked, "Please, when you come down from your rush and are relaxed, I would love to know what each of you felt out there tonight. Also, please tell me what the high point was for each one of you and during which song. I've never personally experienced anything like this, so living it through you is amazing. Thank you for the opportunity."

Felinia, Claire, Sum Tin, and Pussley were all weeping happy, emotional tears and holding each other.

With the rest of the band standing there in awe of what just took place, Max got a call and walked away. It was Hymee, telling him that the crew he sent to Boston just called him and said they had completed the video shoot.

Then Hymee said, "And at the end of the eastern part of the tour, during your hiatus, we would like you all to come back to the studio and look at the footage that was shot today, along with that of the show in Hartford."

Max stood there with another shockwave hitting him! "You taped today's performance, Hymee?"

"We did Max, and your band is on fire! We would love to get all the live footage we possibly can for future album sales. You're doing a great job with these youngsters, and if there's anything you need at all, Max, don't hesitate to ask. I'll see you soon."

Max walked back to his new American musical sensation, known as Pussley Seasons and the Nine Lives Five, and said, "Kids, I believe we're going to sleep well tonight."

In three days, they would be in Albany, and again, the show was already sold out. Pussley and the band were becoming seasoned performers so quickly. Every venue is filled to its maximum, and right now their vocals are about the best in the business. Their songs "Because of Your Fur" and "Walkin' the Edge," are selling wonderfully! "The Sun, My Son, Will Shine"—the live cut—will premiere next month.

The hotel here was older but classy, and the band says the beds are to die for. Although they don't have room service, there is a good restaurant down on the corner. Felinia, Claire Dainty, and Tinkles were the only ones up and so made their way down to the corner. Tinkles, sitting across from the two queens, was enjoying their company. He realized he really liked Claire's personality, so very giving and sincere. Felinia was very attractive but was also more reserved. Still, she found herself to be very comfortable around the others.

Both Claire and Felinia were very happy to be in the band's small circle.

They were enjoying their meal of eggs sunny-side-up and sardine pancakes. The feelings that Claire and Tinkles were getting as they looked at each other while eating and talking were actually taking them to a very pleasant place. Tinkles was very easy to listen to and somewhat philosophical. He always saw the good in everyone and treated others as he wanted to be treated, plus he possessed an amazing musical gift. To Claire, he was very admirable. Several of the stories he told them about how he began with Max were great breakfast conversations. And likewise, Claire shared a few stories of when she and Max were living at home, bringing smiles to Felinia's and Tinkles' faces.

Traffic was heavy with rushing motorists this morning. As they left the restaurant, they waited for the light to change at the corner to cross the street. Suddenly, as they were walking, a motorist who was not paying attention was about to hit Claire! Tinkles, catching this in his peripheral, grabbed Claire and sprang backwards as hard as he could, landing on his back while holding Claire tight. She never touched the pavement! Felinia rushed over to see if everyone was all right. Tinkles' quick reaction had saved Claire, and they knew it. They rose from the street, and Claire went up to Tinkles, gave him a kiss, and said, "I'll never be able to thank you enough."

Tinkles looked into her eyes and said, "You just did."

Felinia was all smiles, seeing the beginning of these two becoming an item.

Upon hearing what happened through Felinia's words, Max hugged Claire tightly and said, "I'm so glad you're okay. I don't know what to think. If we had lost you…" words failed him.

Then Max hugged Tinkles and thanked him for allowing her to keep her lives. This prompted Max to tell the band, "If for any reason you're going out, make sure one of your band mates is with you…don't ever go by yourself."

The band agreed and filed it away within themselves as a lesson learned.

Chapter 21

Pussley was sitting on the veranda, having her kippers and toast, along with her heavy cream, and perusing the paper. She turned the page to the entertainment section ... and there was Tab hugging another queen! She immediately became nauseous, and her heart ached. The paper said she was "an unknown, maybe an adoring fan." It was all speculation. But the fact that he had his paws around her filled Pussley's heart with sadness. Claire and Felinia joined her and immediately asked her what was wrong. She showed the page to both of them, then started crying big tears.

Felinia started going off, saying, "He is a no-good, dirty rotten scoundrel and he doesn't deserve you!"

Claire was a little more reserved and said, "Why don't you wait until you talk with him and find out what he was up to?"

"Oh, you know I will do that!" Pussley said. And until she did, her day was going south, fast. She couldn't finish her breakfast, and she asked to be left alone.

As the girls walked back inside, Tinkles and Kiddy Rock both came out smiling, but in a New York minute, they were frowning for their friend. They had been so used to seeing Pussley with happy tears that this was altogether different.

It made them hurt, also. When she showed them the paper, they shook their heads.

Kiddy said, "He didn't know how good he had it."

Tinkles said, "It doesn't make sense. He knew you would see this."

Within thirty minutes, everyone knew what had happened. They all came to give her hugs and sympathy for her grief.

When Max came out he asked, "What is everyone doing out here?"

Someone showed him the paper. He looked at it for several minutes, took the paper with him, and walked out the door into the hallway. He walked down and knocked on Philly's door ... bam, bam, bam!

Cornwallis opened it and said, "Good morning, Mr. Maxwell."

"Good morning, young man," he said. Would you go grab Philly for me, please?"

"Sure thing, Mr. Maxwell."

Philly came through one of the room doors with Tab right behind him and walked up to Max.

He said, "Good morning. What can I do for you?"

Max practically ripped the paper open and said, "Can you please explain this?"

The two toms looked at the picture, then looked at each other and started laughing! This pushed a button in Max, and he got right in Tab's face. With a very menacing growl, he said to the both of them, "Choose your words wisely."

Philly spoke first. "Hold on there, big fella … it's not what you think!"

"You don't want to know what I'm thinking right now, Philly!"

Tab got between them and said, "Mr. Maxwell, that picture of me and that woman isn't me going behind Pussley's back. That's me hugging my sister who came to see me!"

Philly piped in, "Yeah, Max. That's his sister. She came in and surprised him! The media never seems to get it right."

Max sat down on the couch and sighed, saying, "Oh my goodness. I am so relieved. Let me get Pussley down here so you can explain it to her. She needs to hear it from you, Tab."

Five minutes later, Pussley entered. She walked in while sobbing and asked, "Tab, why?"

Tab replied, "Kitten, it's not what you think! The paper got it wrong."

Pussley shot back, "Don't they say a picture is worth a thousand words?"

Philly made his exit and left the two of them there.

Tab sat next to Pussley on the couch, looked into her eyes, and said, "I would never treat you so disrespectfully. I think the world of you."

"What in the world are you talking about, Tab? In this world, my heart is broken!"

"Pussley, in our world, that is my sister, Muffins." She came to see me yesterday and we met at a cafe while photographers were taking my picture. They happened to catch one of me hugging my sister, who was trying to surprise me. She's staying on the floor below us. Would you like to go meet her?"

She reached out and hugged him hard. "I'm so very sorry, I thought …"

Tab spoke, "Don't say anything. In this business, it happens often. But I was raised old school, and that is to treat felines the way you want to be treated."

The kiss he gave her took away all of her worries, turned her frown to a smile, and left her feeling a little embarrassed.

Tab spoke up. "You still want to go meet her?"

"Not like this, Tab, I'm a mess!"

"Well, put yourself back together and we'll all go out for a nice seafood dinner tonight. And Pussley…just remember that you're still my queen."

Chapter 22

The morning of the Albany show started slowly with a light breakfast of sunny-sided eggs, flounder bites, and English muffins with lots of butter and flavored heavy cream. It was always welcome and always enjoyable. After the meal, Tinkles asked Claire Dainty if she would like to go for a walk, to which she said, "I would like that."

When the doors closed in the elevator on the way down, Claire slipped her paw into Tinkles'. He looked at her and gave her a sweet little kiss, which immediately set her to purring.

Tab called Pussley to say that he would see her at the sound check at two o'clock this afternoon, and that after the show they would all go out to dinner.

"Yes, I am looking forward to that, Tab," Pussley said.

Pussley was feeling silly because of her reaction the other day, but it seemed that nobody held it against her. It was already forgotten as just a tabloid's erroneous reporting. Pussley's heart was wide open and ready for love. It was bound to happen, but with Tab's transparency, it would now continue with smooth sailing ahead.

Growing up in Purrville, Pussley dated several musicians, but they never gave her the respect or the real affection that she was looking for, so she mainly stayed to herself or with her musical friends and acquaintances. It was safer that way … she didn't have to feel vulnerable. For a young queen growing up on her own, that's a scary place to be. Although she would have liked to have had a steady boyfriend, it just seemed that the cost was too high for risking her heart in an unsure relationship.

At her birth, there were three in her litter and sadly, Pussley never really knew her mother or father. She was adopted quickly and never realized she had two brothers who were all split up around the same time. When she was a teen, she overheard her owner speaking with his brother, who had apparently adopted one of her brothers! This set in motion a desire to find him, but that wouldn't happen for another year.

Pussley had always enjoyed singing, and when asked if she would enter a singing contest by her now reunited friend, Felinia, a nervous Pussley stood on a stage and belted out her first song in front of others. To her amazement, she was received with much applause, which she enjoyed. Thus began the search for the next contest, and at that next event, Pussley had sung her way to becoming the winner! As a result, she was asked by the band known as Keep Your Pause Off if she would sing with them, which she was happy to do!

Their songwriter, Kit, was talking to Pussley one evening during a break and mentioned that his owner, Jack Seasons, happened to be the brother of Pussley's owner, John. And so, her wish of finding her brother was realized, and the two became inseparable.

Still new to singing in public, this is where she would grow in confidence and become comfortable in finding her voice and range.

Playing locally for several years and having honed her vocal abilities, it allowed her to explore the notes she heard so often within her mind. This gave her a unique take on songs, which resulted in a growing local and loyal fan base. Unfortunately, this all came to an end when gossip got back to her of the lies that some of the band members were telling about her. This severely broke their trust and destroyed their relationships.

But happily, in less than a month, Pussley caught wind of the audition that Max was holding, which brought her to this happy place in which she now found herself. She firmly believed many things happened for a reason.

Pussley and the band arrived right at two for the sound check. With Kinfur ending their time slot, it was The Nine Lives' turn. Tab grabbed a beautiful bouquet of flowers from behind Cornwallis's drum set and walked over to Pussley. He handed it to her, gave her a kiss, and said, "I'm sorry that you thought I was over you. Nothing could be further from the truth."

Pussley again cried happy tears.

She sang the two songs that they played for their check powerfully, clearly in her zone. The band knew it would be a good night.

Chapter 23

The limos pulled up to the rear of The Cat's Cradle, a five-thousand-seat auditorium that would be filled to capacity with an adoring audience.

Backstage, Tinkles had asked Philly if they could try several of the new tunes that had been written by the band. Philly's reply was, "I have no problem with that, Tinkles. Give 'em what you got."

"Thank you for supporting us, Mr. Shnizlestix."

"Worry about nothing, kids, you've earned it."

Tinkles told the band the two songs they had been working with in the hotels were going to be tried out on this Albany audience. Because their vibe was so strong and their musicianship secure, there was no hesitation from any of them, just a desire to see how the audience would receive them. The first number would be played halfway through the set. It had an up-tempo bluesy feel, created from Catz's love for his early influences. It started like this:

"The Nine Lives Bop"

You came strutting my way, playing your game
Making me ask you for your sweet kitty name
Acting hard to get and couldn't care less
If a cat like me, I must confess
Showed a bona fide interest in your style
The wink you gave me, your hint of demure
Sent my tail shooting skyward, with an audible purr
And when my paw touched yours, without
     pulling away
I knew that we two would be able to play

Chorus
The Nine Lives Bop is a lot of fun
Touching paws, and becoming one
A real romance with a cat's meow
Come dance with me, and I'll show you how

An item is what we need to be
Me loving you, and you loving me
We'll set the world before us ablaze
Swinging together in this new dance craze

Chorus
The Nine Lives Bop is a lot of fun
Touching paws, and becoming one
A real romance with a cat's meow
Come dance with me, and I'll show you how

When they finished, the audience wailed in controlled chaos!

Kinfur's members said, "That was one catchy tune!"

Max admitted he had only heard bits and pieces, but still, they all agreed this was going to score high on the charts. Pussley was rapidly becoming America's kitty cat sweetheart.

The second number, a ballad sung by all four vocalists, filled the room with emotion and tears of release from understanding and sympathetic fans.

This song was called "Maybe Too Young."

"Maybe Too Young"

I'm making bread and I don't know why
When my nails extend, it just makes me cry
Maybe too young, from litter to home
Never knowing my parents, feeling so all alone
Brings me to seek all the love that I can
From places I shouldn't, and tom's I should ban
With my life so uncertain, and no anchor that holds
I'm tossed to and fro, as my days do unfold

Chorus
Maybe too young to go it alone
Just weeks and I'm leaving for some other home
I'm happy for those who can see Mama's eyes
Curling up in a ball, give her all of your of sighs

After the show, the band was asked if they would sign some autographs by the venue's owner, and they all said, "Sure!"

When they came out to the front of the stage, there were hundreds of new Nine Lives Five fans waiting for their chance to meet their new faves. As the band was moving through the line, Pussley was approached by a beautiful young feline named Kitty Littré who had opened a large binder full of the band's stage shots, pictures of them from Purrville, even some of them when they were kittens! There were also copies of all the tweets and messages from thankful and adoring fans.

Pussley asked her, "How did you collect all of this?"

Kitty replied, "I've been following your career since you were singing with Keep Your Pause Off. I was in the audience on the day you sang in that contest."

Pussley was floored. She had never seen her early life chronicled like this—so flattering and nostalgic. Kitty asked her for the opportunity to meet with her because she wanted to talk about starting the Pussley Seasons and the Nine Lives Five Fan Club!

Pussley turned around, and the entire band was surrounding her, smiling and trying to turn the pages to see more. The thought of having a fan club tickled them, so telling Kitty to come to their hotel room this evening, where she and Pussley could talk, was a big "okay."

Pussley was caught off guard, but said smiling, "I guess I'll see you tonight."

She looked across the room and saw Kinfur signing autographs. She waved to Tab, who smiled, and she was then escorted to the limos. On the way back to the hotel, Pussley was thinking about the thousands upon thousands of adoring felines wanting to know what she and the band were doing, and it caused her to shake her head in disbelief, thinking *how silly fame can be*.

Chapter 24

The two bands boarded their buses, driven by Philly's two uncles, Bobby and Vinny Boombots. The Nine Lives' queens followed behind in the rented luxury sedan to maintain propriety and avoid gossip, but it was also a great time for Pussley to work with Sum Tin on their harmonies. They would spend half the day driving to the next show in Buffalo at Rocky's Music Hall, which has the capacity for six thousand five hundred dogs and cats. Like all their past venues, it would be filled to the brim tomorrow evening.

Tinkles was writing a song for his new kitty, Claire Dainty, or as he likes to call her, "his pretty little kitty from the city." Kit was busy writing some more ideas from Tinkles' suggestions. Yanx was beating on a bucket to Catz and Kiddy playing on their acoustics, being as creative as they ever were. The band was surely in a zone, and their chemistry was only getting better.

Claire Dainty was telling her new friends about the kiss that Tinkles had given her, making them all meow loudly with laughter and easily opening the door for other stories. Pussley revealed details of her romantic day on the town with Tab. Felinia mentioned that she noticed Kiddy Rock looking at her in a way that made her feel special and not like just the runner—and that she liked it.

Sum Tin, looking sad, mentioned that she had no one. "I haven't noticed one tom looking at me." Having said that, the remaining three huddled around her with hugs, kissing her forehead and letting her know that they loved her, and that she would never be alone.

Pussley looked right into her eyes and said, "Sweetie, there is someone out there that you will meet, and one day soon, you will fall in love."

"Oh, I so want to believe you," Sum Tin said.

The Kinfur bus had another vibe going. The bass and guitar players were talking amongst themselves when their petty jealousies erupted once again. This time, the bass player even pushed Cornwallis. With his professional demeanor and commitment to managing his emotions, Cornwallis stated, "Alex, if you mention this again, we will drop you off at the next small town and you will have to find your own way back. We will mail you your things. Oh, and Alex, remember this—If you ever touch me in anger again, your career using your paws to earn a living will be over. Do you understand?"

It was obvious to all that Cornwallis was indeed the general, not to mention Philly's favorite nephew. To disrespect him equated to immediate termination. Alex went to reside in the back of the bus, pouting with his paws crossed but saying nothing.

Max and Philly were being driven in Kitty Corner's limo by Philly's half-brother, Carlo Gaga. They were talking of the old days and how they thank God daily for making it out of there with all of their lives intact.

Max got a phone call from Puddin Cup, telling him that the cases of his merchandise—with the band's logos in three different sizes and colors—would be waiting in their hotel room when they arrive in Buffalo. This caused Max to roar, scaring Philly in the process. Max hung up, apologized to Philly, and told him everything that they ordered would be in Buffalo waiting for them. All Max could do was to sit back and say, "Outstanding!"

Philly was thinking to himself *It is much better having Max as a friend than an enemy.*

Playing these large cities with a band as big as Kinfur has Pussley and her band waiting for the other shoe to drop. In such a short time, life has done a one-eighty; a complete turnaround. Anything on this scale was usually just dreamed of, read about in magazines, or seen on social media…but to actually be part of a working rock band that people are paying to see, read about, and wanting to know what they're doing … well, as the band says, "It feels like we really are in a movie!"

So … action!

Chapter 25

The band pulls up in Buffalo at the Hotel Troubadour. Its old-world charm makes the band feel special and important. Built in the 1800s, its architectural details make it one of Buffalo's finest establishments and well-suited for up-and-coming feline rock stars.

The very first thing the band did once in their rooms was to call for room service. The long haul here had left them famished, and they needed their energy for tomorrow's show. Max arrived to see trays full of smelts, shrimp, and fish cakes, with two flavors of heavy cream.

This left Max saying, "I'm really liking this touring thing!"

The band, eating and laughing, agreed with him. They were already looking forward to tomorrow afternoon's sound check.

Tinkles gave Claire a hug, and Max saw that she hugged him back. Realizing that his two favorite cool cats had feelings for each other made him smile.

Pussley was in her room talking on the phone with Tab, already making plans for the day after the show to see the town. Felinia and Kiddie Rock were singing a song that they remembered from years back, smiling and having a good time. Catz and

Sum Tin were working on harmonies for a new song Catz was writing. Yanx had his headphones on, listening to a jazz drummer's tutorial. Max, taking it all in and seeing that the family was enjoying some happy together time, made him smile a big smile. He thought, *Enjoy this while you can, kids, for tomorrow evening is all business, and business is good!*

Max got a call from Hymee, telling him that their album, "… has just gone platinum! It is now the fastest rising album in the country … or that we have ever produced! When the band is done with their tour, there will be a huge bash for all of you to attend. The media, industry execs, and the top mags will all be there to congratulate you. What do you have to say about that, Max?"

"I don't know what to say, Hymee. Except thank you for making this all possible! Because of you and Kitty Corner Records, we are all living our best lives."

"Max, I believe that feeling is mutual. There's not a day that goes by that I don't receive a call from my peers in this business asking me what my secret is. The only thing I can tell them is, you've got to have talent. You and I have happened upon six youngsters with an abundance of it!"

"Indeed, we have, Hymee. Indeed, we have." Max also said, "We'll see you soon, and again, thanks for everything."

"You're so very welcome, Max. Goodbye."

Max was on top of the world, and he had to share it with those who made it possible. Max called everyone into the living area.

"What's up, Maxi?" said Tinkles.

Everyone was now eager to hear what he had to say.

"Kit kats, I just received a call from the label telling me your album is the fastest rising album in the country! It's already gone platinum! And at the end of this tour, there'll be a huge party to congratulate and acknowledge your wonderful talents and beautiful music."

With that, Pussley and Tinkles both started weeping. A beautiful moment for their achievements thus far, causing Tinkles to say, "Maxi, we're going to have another album's worth of music when we get back."

"The label knows that Tinkles," Max said. "They will already be waiting for us to lay down our tracks on wax."

The band laughed, meowed, and purred at that.

Then Max asked Yanx to grab one of the large boxes in the foyer and bring it over. Max told everyone, "I think you're going to like this."

All eyes were upon him when he reached in and pulled out the very first Pussley Seasons and the Nine Lives Five silk-screened shirt in a beautiful teal color. Everyone moved in quickly, wanting to put one on. Even Max found his size. A knock came on the door, and in came Cutie Patootie and PQ with all the freshly dry-cleaned suits and outfits for tomorrow night's show. Yanx got his box of various-colored headbands along with two more sleeveless vests. This band was looking sharp no matter where they were.

Max then made a call to a local contractor who would set up several tables and racks to show off the band's new merchandise that afternoon. T-shirts, hoodies, photos, key rings, and even plastic cups, all with the band's logo, were ready for sale. Another key element was now in place for The Nine Lives Five musical troupe.

Chapter 26

The band walked into Rocky's that afternoon, ready to give their sound check. Today they would go first, and while they were setting up on stage and taking their places, Max asked Felinia and Claire Dainty if they would like to sell the band's merchandise this evening. Both pretty queens said that it would be fun and that they would be glad to help out.

"Don't forget to wear your band shirts tonight," Max said, walking away.

He then checked on the contractor's progress. His workmen already had the wooden structures and tables set up nicely and were now working on the electrical feeds and coding the point-of-sale to the cash register.

Felinia and Claire Dainty were very impressed by how fast and professional Max Maxwell, their manager, was at getting things done. Having walked back into the stage area, Pussley and Sum Tin were upset that their mics kept going in and out and were nervous about the evening.

Max went to the two toms at the board and asked if there was going to be a problem.

"We'll have it all cleared up," they said.

"I hope so," said Max. "This is supposed to be the time during which anything like this is cleared up!"

Other than that glitch, everything sounded good. The band would be back in six hours with a truckload of merchandise, a belly full of anticipation, and eager to please their audience.

The facility's backline had their two new toms disconnect the faulty mic wires to replace them with new ones, but somehow these two bumbling feline buffoons managed to reconnect the two old wires and took away the two new ones, setting things up for a possible showtime disaster.

Rocky's started filling up an hour and a half before the start of the show. The band and entourage had already arrived. Sum Tin and Felinia neatly filled the tables and cubbies with merchandise, making it resemble a small department store.

Max was happy, and noticeably as big as Kinfur was, their merchandise area was a shambles. Shirts not folded nicely, novelty items thrown together in baskets, not all sizes were available—it looked, well … cheap! Just unbecoming for a band as popular and admired as they are.

But of course, this came down to the management style of Philly, which is a bit sloppy at times. Philly, a very likable tom who came from a very large family back in Purrville, was the middle kitten in a litter of seven and grew up in a canine-dominated area of Purrville. Sometimes he had to fight for a meal. He never received much love from his mother or siblings. He gravitated towards the City Bobcats early on. As a pseudo family, it's where he met Maxipuss Maxwell from another Chapter at a large rally. They became friends and occasionally got the chance to ride together. At that time, things were starting to heat up with a rival motorcycle club known as The Crooked Jaguars, which wanted to move into the area and take over.

This forced Maxipuss and Philly to represent the City Bobcats in throwing down with their rivals. The situation was getting bloodier, and that's when Max's sisters stepped in and pleaded with him to come away, citing that the needs of the family should come before gang violence. Listening to reason, Max walked away, telling Philly it was no longer fun but a struggle to survive and that it really didn't have to be. Also, he didn't want to be surrounded by the drama of it all. Several weeks later, Philly came to his senses and walked away, as well.

Philly moved into hotel management with help from one of his uncles. He had done a complete one-eighty from his previous lifestyle. In his fifth successful year, a very popular rock band known as Nightwatch—out of New York—came to stay with them for a show they would be giving in two nights. When their manager arrived, he was noticeably inebriated and acting obnoxiously. He was completely unable to manage his band. This made Philly feel he should call the label or something. With no one to guide the band, he felt he should fill them in on some details. After all, it was Kitty Corner Records that booked their headlining band.

So, when a young Hymee the Himalayan heard of this, he was exceedingly upset and asked Philly if he would go up to their rooms and tell the manager that he was fired.

He also made Philly an offer for the position as manager of the band Nightwatch, knowing that he was already a successful hotel manager. Philly accepted the proposal and became Nightwatch's new manager.

Over the years, the band had several personnel changes and evolved into the band we now know as Kinfur.

Chapter 27

"Start time in five! Everyone, take your places," says the house stage manager.

Tab walks up and gives Pussley a wonderful kiss, saying, "Knock them out, sweetness!"

Hearing that, Pussley throws her paws around Tab and says, "I will do just that!"

The countdown sounds ... "Three, two, one, lights!"

The band kicks it in with "Walkin' the Edge." Immediately, Catz signals to the sound engineers at the board to turn up the volume in his monitor, but nothing changes. In between chords, he touches his ear as he's looking at them ... but still nothing changes. He deals with his frustration as best he can and continues to play.

Sum Tin notices that her vocal harmony is going in and out with Pussley every time she touches the mic. This causes her to look at the soundboard techs and point to her microphone ... but no stagehands appear.

They finish the number and go right into the next one. Once again, Sum Tin's mic is intermittent, causing her panic and frustration. Even Pussley turned her head to see what was going on. Catz, noticing what was happening with her mic, motions for her to come sing through his mic, and he would sing with her when he had to.

So, at a point where Pussley was singing solo, Sum Tin walked across the stage to Catz's mic and their beautiful vocal harmonies returned with Pussley looking over their way smiling. The next tune was the song Catz wrote, so all four would be singing this one. Just when the song started to unfold, Pussley's mic hit a dead spot. Just like that—nothing! Thankfully, Tinkles, Catz, and Sum Tin could be heard. Pussley, not missing a beat, shut her mic off and walked across the stage, smiling over to Catz and Sum Tin to complete their beautifully harmonized number.

The audience went crazy. The shortsighted stage gaffe turned out to be a happy accident. Tab, seeing these issues, took his wireless mic and had it synced with The Nine Live's sound. Then he ran back through the crowd and went behind the curtain to the side of the stage. Before the next song began, amidst all of the wonderful applause, Tab came out on stage and handed Pussley his wireless mic. He kissed her cheek and walked off.

The crowd went into a frenzy, thinking that it was all part of the show. Backstage, Max hugged Tab and thanked him for being so cool-headed. But Max, being upset, was really giving the stage manager the business. He pointed out the completely unprofessional way their backline left the microphone situation and said that this would be the first and last time they would ever play here. The band's set came to an end, and they bowed to a roaring, appreciative crowd.

The problems had been solved, and their part of the show was successfully done.

Pussley handed the mic to Tab, gave him a kiss, and said, "Thank you so much! I must repay you for your kindness. This time you saved us!"

"One paw washes the other," Tab said and went to get ready for their entrance.

Catz came over to the stage manager and said loudly, "Why was my monitor not turned up for me? And what was going on with those microphones? I thought they would be taken care of … or, so we were told."

The manager had nothing further to say. He was already completely embarrassed and knew just who's grandcat wasn't going to be working there in the morning.

The band promptly rode back to the hotel. On the drive back, the band realized that some quick moves had avoided a catastrophe. Thanks to the quick thinking of Catz and Tab, the night was an overall success.

Last night's performance, although tricky with a few obstacles, was another notch in their belt of success. Despite the mistakes made by the sound crew, their blunders actually created a dynamic that the band hadn't heard before. Tinkles, Catz, and Sum Tin standing together and singing into one mic created a blend that was full, rich, and very organic.

This prompted Tinkles to have a conversation with Max, saying that for their next performance coming up in Cleveland, they wanted a boom mic hanging overhead for Catz's song, "The Sun, My Son, Will Shine."

Max replied, "That's a wonderful idea, Tinkles. It sounded great and the audience liked it. There was a moment of a family-like atmosphere that I believe the audience related to, so we'll make that a standard for that number."

"You're the best, Maxi," said Tinkles.

Everyone practically slept through breakfast. Pussley got up, bathed, and was getting ready for her day-date with Tab. They were now very aware that photographers would catch up with them. Still, it was their time, and she didn't even want to think about them. She just wanted to enjoy their precious time together.

When Tinkles got up, he made a plate of breakfast items, poured a cup of heavy cream, and knocked on the door to Claire Dainty's room. A voice came from within saying, "Come in … it's open."

And there was Claire, lying down. Tinkles walked toward her and said, "Breakfast in bed, my dear?"

"Oh my! This is so sweet! No one has ever done this for me before. Thank you, Tinkles."

He bent over, kissed her lips, and looking into her eyes, he said, "This can happen as often as you would like."

At that, Claire meowed and said, "I'm going to take you up on that."

Before he left, he asked her if she'd like to go for a walk with him a little later in the day. She answered, "It's a date, tiger."

Max received a call from Hymee saying that the Mayor of Buffalo wanted to have dinner with the band this evening at C'est Un Endroit Pour Chats (It's A Cat's Place).

"His daughter is a big fan and would love to meet the band. Plus, it would be a great photo op for the band to be seen during a night out on the town."

Maxi said, "That sounds great, Hymee. But I have one favor to ask of you."

"Sure, Max, what is it?"

"I would also like Kinfur to be invited as guests. Last night there were technical difficulties that we had no control over, and their lead singer, Tab, saved the evening with some quick thinking. I would like to thank him for that."

"Sounds simple enough, Max," said Hymee. "I'll get back to you soon."

Catz, playing on his acoustic, came across a lovely progression and was getting a really good feeling about it while getting it into his paws. He scribbled some words down, then he came and asked Sum Tin if she would harmonize with him.

She said, "Yes, of course."

The sound of their duet was an instant hit!

No other voices were necessary; the simplicity was perfect. The band got to hear it before lunch, and it elevated everyone, knowing that they would add this awesome song to their already strong chain of up-and-coming hits. Everyone was legitimately happy with their new dynamic duo. Sum Tin was all smiles, as was Catz. While everyone was talking, Catz put his paw around Sum Tin's shoulder. To him, it felt natural and Sum Tin … well, she wasn't going anywhere.

Pussley, grinning with tears in her eyes, left to go meet Tab down in the lobby.

Chapter 28

The limo pulled up in front, Carlo got out, and opened the door for Pussley and Tab to get in.

"Where to, sir?" he asked.

"Downtown, Carlo," said Tab.

The slow drive downtown was very nice. Sitting next to each other while holding paws and occasionally kissing was just what the doctor ordered. Love, when viewed in the right light, can keep you grounded and influence your whole outlook. Currently, their future is looking bright. Tab asked Pussley if she would humor him for several moments, and he had Carlo pull up in front of the record store.

Pussley said, "What do you have on your mind?"

"I'd like to take a look and see how your record is doing."

"Oh," said Pussley.

With Pussley happily surprised, they walked in with sunglasses on to allow them a few moments of anonymity. Standing in the doorway, looking over the room, they noticed Pussley's album displayed at the side of the front counter along with their promotional posters. They walked over to the counter where Tab pointed and asked the clerk, "Is this record any good?"

Holding the album in his hands, the young clerk replied, "I've never seen an album fly off the shelves as fast as this one. It's like every song on there is one of their greatest hits." He turned around, pushed a button, and the turntable's needle dropped down on an open copy of it. "Walkin' the Edge" started playing. At that moment, Tab and Pussley heard half the people in the store start singing the tune.

Tab took his glasses off and asked Pussley to remove hers as well. Then he asked her, "Why don't you sing with them?"

Pussley had come to love impromptu moments, so she started singing the song with her passion, causing all eyes to look up toward the counter. Actually seeing Pussley Seasons in person, singing one of their new faves so spontaneously, was surreal for the customers. By now, the entire store was singing with her. When the song came to an end, everyone in the store clapped their paws wildly. They came up to her and Tab, asking for their autographs.

Everyone in the store that morning received Tab's and Pussley's autographs along with dozens of pictures taken before they got back into the limo to continue on their way for the day.

"Oh, Tab, that was so much fun!" Pussley gushed.

"I thought you might like that, honey," Tab said.

She practically jumped into his lap and put her paws around his neck, kissing his entire face. Tab was laughing, meowing, and purring with Pussley smiling and giggling. The whole moment was wonderful. This alone was worth the trip to Buffalo.

The car stopped at a little out-of-the-way bistro called The Calico Cafe, where they dined on escargot and broiled sea bass. No one recognized them. No one bothered them. It was just the two of them having a wonderful lunch. Just two regular felines in love, enjoying each other's company.

Hymee called Max and told him everything was a go. "Philly couldn't say enough nice things about you, Max. I don't know what you're doing out there, but it certainly is the right thing. Oh, and Max … whatever pictures are taken—I would appreciate it if you would send copies my way."

"Sure, Hymee, I'd be glad to."

Both bands were looking forward to the evening's dinner, rubbing shoulders with the mayor and some other prominent felines. This was something that they had never done before, but right now, being more popular than they already were, boosted the way they saw themselves. Yes, they were rock bands, but they were well-known and well-liked rock bands. And that was the name of that tune.

The mayor was a corpulent and jovial feline … telling jokes, and laughing loudly, which was indeed infectious and made for a wonderful time dining out. Autographs were freely given to anyone who asked, and dozens of pictures were taken throughout the night. This evening allowed the two bands to be who they were as cats. No egos, no agendas, just everyone coming together and being happy in the moment.

Max stood up and asked everyone for a moment so he could speak. He thanked Tab for his quick thinking, which resolved what could have been a catastrophe into a blessing. He also thanked Philly and the mayor for making this pleasant evening a reality.

The mayor responded by saying, "You're so very welcome!"

In front of everyone, Philly now said, "You are a class act, Max!"

Both bands held up their glasses of cream and in unison said, "Hear, hear!"

The mayor's daughter got to take pictures with just her and the bands, then got hugs from Pussley and Tab, which left them all with pretty smiles.

With the evening coming to an end, Catz and Sum Tin went outside to get some air. While Sum Tin was saying how wonderful the night was, Catz put his paws around her snuggly and kissed her—oh, so long—that she melted in his paws. They didn't want the moment to end, but approaching voices told them that they had to. Although from that moment on, they saw each other much differently, wondering why this hadn't happened sooner.

The bands were exiting the doors and seeing Catz's paw around Sum Tin made the queens of Nine Lives come over to them and give all of them hugs. For everyone involved, it was one of their best nights.

Chapter 29

The Band arrived at the hotel in Cleveland and walked in like they were family. The bellhop was waiting to take them to their rooms. There was talking, laughing, and an overall feeling of well-being. They just knew that this was where they belonged. Being a successful rock band with hits sure had its perks—wonderful rooms, glorious food, beautiful clothing, people wanting your autograph and picture! It would be quite easy to get into mischief, but with Max's integrity and the behavior of these youngsters, that type of lifestyle wasn't a goal. Making great music, giving it away to adoring fans, and seeing the world had its merits in their feline hearts.

Catz's song with Sum Tin was perfected and would be played at the small arena in Cleveland tomorrow night. This beautiful duet for a heartfelt love song will leave listeners wanting more. They believed this would be an upcoming crown jewel in the band's treasured and growing list of melodies. The sweetness of Sum Tin's harmony blended with Catz's soft whisper of a German accent would leave the listeners wanting to sing it to their loved ones.

With all the writing and creativity for new songs going on, Tinkles was right in saying they would have another album ready to record during their hiatus.

Max was all too happy to be looking over them, keeping them safe, and watching them enjoy their new lives.

That morning, Claire Dainty would be with Philly, going over all of the itinerary: the load-in, soundcheck, dressing rooms, food and beverage, appearance time, and all the locations of everything. Claire was a quick study, and Philly liked that. She had good ideas and great common sense. Philly knew she was someone he could work well with.

Once everything was in place and secure, Claire would double down with the new venture that she and Felinia were handling. They would open up their new Nine Lives Boutique ... or at least that's what they were calling it. As in Buffalo, boxes of merch would be waiting in the hotel rooms to be sold pre- and post-concert. It was a nice source of additional income and was practically selling out at every show. Claire was also keeping the books for that. Max had found a gold mine in his sister's talents.

In addition, now she and Tinkles had found love. The only sad thing about that is that the whole feline world couldn't experience it too. But again, not everybody possesses the talent that led this band to this place in their lives. Felinia was given enough money to buy strings for Catz and Kiddy Rock. The music store was approximately five blocks away, and if she could wait for an hour, the limo would be able to take her. But since the guys needed to make sure their instruments were in tip-top shape quickly, she said she would just walk to pick up everything they needed. As she reached the second block of her walk, she noticed two strangers who were still back a ways, but were gaining ground.

The only two numbers that she had in her phone were Max's and Kiddy Rock's. She tried calling Max but did not get an answer. Even though she increased her pace, these two suspicious characters were getting closer, and she was getting nervous. When three blocks away, she finally connected with Kiddy Rock, telling him what was happening.

Kiddy Rock ran out the door, telling Pussley to alert everyone to what was happening on Felinia's way to the music store.

Pussley called Max, and he answered, saying, "What's up, kid?"

"Felinia is three blocks away, heading to the music store, and there are two cats after her…she is very scared."

Max let out a roar so loud that it hurt Pussley's ears through the phone.

Max called Philly and told him to have the limo out in front ASAP because Felinia is about to get mugged halfway to the music store.

"The driver is busy, buddy. I'll grab it and be there in two minutes!"

"Thanks, Philly, I'll be here waiting."

By the time Kiddy Rock could see a block and a half up, there were four thug cats surrounding Felinia! He quickened his pace. He knew he would pounce on the biggest one without fear or care … all that mattered was keeping Felinia from getting hurt.

At half a block away, the would-be thieves saw Kiddy coming and had two of their own turn to face him, waiting for the clash. At that same moment, a large limousine with squealing tires barreled towards the impending violence. Passing Kiddy Rock and screeching the brakes, both managers jumped out. Philly and Max pounced on her would-be attackers!

Max grabbed the first one that threw a punch at him, grabbed his paw and snapped it, causing him to wail like a little kitten, then run away. Philly threw himself into two of them, knocking them both down, kicking, punching, and clawing till they were both out cold. One remained, the biggest one. He was going after Felinia, but Kiddy Rock, in full stride, launched his muscular body upon his head, digging in with all of his strength and using his nails like daggers. He brought the beast down to his hind legs. Max grabbed Felinia, asking if she was hurt.

"No, sir, just shaking like a leaf. They were just telling me to give them all of my money when they saw Kiddy running hard and heard your tires squealing. Philly went up to the big cat and, with a full swing of his paw, he knocked him out cold."

"Well done, Philly! And you, too, Kiddy! That was very brave… ready to take on all four of them," Max said.

"That felt like old times, biker dude," chuckled Philly.

"Indeed, it did, Tabby One!"

They both laughed hard.

Then Max said to Kiddy, "Hey buddy, let's all get in the car and go to the music store. Philly and I will stay out here, while you two go get the things you need."

In the store, Felinia thanked Kiddy Rock for coming to her rescue so quickly. She threw her paws around him and kissed him, saying, "Thank you for being my hero."

With that, he replied, "There is nothing I wouldn't do for you, Felinia."

She huddled in Kiddy Rock's paws all the way back.

Max said to Philly, "Thanks for being there for me."

"I got your back, big cat."

Philly dropped them off at the front and went to park the limo.

Upon their arrival, the entire band met them at the door, asking if she was okay. The queens took her away immediately to the refuge of their rooms, wanting to hear all with no detail left out.

Max told his version to the rest of the band. Everyone thanked Max and congratulated Kiddy Rock, calling him one brave mountain lion.

Chapter 30

"The stage at the Millennium Indoor Coliseum will hold eight thousand, five hundred screaming fans this evening. The band will take the stage at 8:00 p.m. The sound check is at 2:00 p.m. The bands are less than 2 miles from the Millennium. Kinfur's sound check is at 1:00 p.m., so the limo will drop them off first, then come back for Pussley Seasons and the Nine Lives band."

"I got it!" said Claire Dainty, speaking to Philly.

She knocked on her brother's door and went in to show him the itinerary.

Max said, "This really comes easily to you, doesn't it, Claire?"

"Sort of, I guess."

"Well, keep doing what you're doing, Sis, and we'll all ride this till the wheels fall off."

Max ordered room service lunch for everyone—tuna sandwiches, shrimp cocktails, catnip-filled chocolates, and three flavors of heavy cream. Everything a growing rock band needed to keep smiling. With the two trays of food practically wiped out, the band had an hour to take a catnap before leaving.

Kiddy Rock and Felinia were walking paw-in-paw down the hallways of the hotel while talking and getting to know each other. Kiddy Rock was very happy with her. She turned out to be a real sweetie. She's a little more reserved than the others, but he's finding out she has a heart of gold.

The sound check at the Millennium went smoothly and sounded amazing. The last song that was played through the system was Catz's duet with Sum Tin, and the band believes this will be one of their best songs ever:

"A Gift Divine"

You've become a living part of me
You feed me with inspiration
And quench my thirst when I drink you in
With the touch of your paw
And your eyes meeting mine
The vision I behold
Has us sharing our sweet time
We have this love
We have our time
To build a life that's yours and mine
Having all that comes, whether rain or shine
We embrace the day
A gift divine

Walking through the lobby up to the rooms is a black cat who is playing one of their songs, "Walkin' the Edge" on saxophone. He is truly a seasoned player, and when he sees the band, he stops and introduces himself as Homer Randolph. He asks if it would ever be possible to play a few numbers with them because he knows all of their material and thinks the world of it.

Tinkles is intrigued and asks this dark Bombay cool cat to wait there in the lobby.

As Max and the band close the elevator doors and are traveling upward, Tinkles asks them if they would like Homer to play with them on the song "Walkin' the Edge" this evening.

"It's obvious he's quite talented," says Tinkles.

"I don't mind," says Catz. "I can give him my solo time plus a few extra measures."

Kiddy Rock says, "I'd like to hear it."

Pussley and Sum Tin are also okay with it.

"Sounds crazy cool, kit kats," said Max.

So, as the band poured out into the hallway, Tinkles stayed behind and went back down to tell Homer of his opportunity.

The band arrived an hour before showtime. Claire and Felinia went to their boutique. They were enjoying the constant rush of fans who desired to have merchandise featuring their band.

Pussley and Tab took a few moments to sneak out back for kisses and catching up. Catz and Sum Tin were going over their song a cappella. Tinkles met with Homer, filling him in on his cue to come out on stage. Max and Philly were speaking with the stage manager. All three were laughing and getting along well. Kiddy Rock and Yanx were talking about the new set of drums Yanx was looking at with Felinia by his side.

Then Cutie Patootie called everyone into the dressing rooms for wardrobe and makeup.

The sound of excited fans filling the Millennium was giving everyone their evening adrenaline rush. What's even more exciting would be trying out new songs in front of the audience. For the band tonight, it should be golden.

Chapter 31

Lights up—curtains open—the band hits the audience with one of their heavier numbers. Already, the audience has jumped out of their seats singing, "I've Got To Carry On," a blues rock number that Tinkles wrote. It's got a catchy chorus and a nice hook.

Volumes are perfect and the mics work great! It's different when your backline is completely professional. Unlike when you've hired your lazy grandcat, who doesn't know the first thing about what he's doing! All shows here at the Millennium are presented the way they're supposed to be, optimized for complete fan and band satisfaction. Attention to detail is of utmost importance, and there were always two stagehands, one on each side, in case anyone should need assistance.

Pussley is talking to the crowd and asks for a round of applause to welcome their guest saxophonist, Homer Randolph. And because she asked for it, she got it. Eighty-five hundred screaming fans were waiting to hear what they were going to do.

Earlier backstage, Tinkles had spoken with Homer and told him that his solo could come when Catz usually takes his. "If you'd like to freelance in the beginning of the song, and if you're feeling it through the tune, believing you have something to say, go ahead and blow."

"I can't thank you enough, Mr. Tinkles, for this shot."

"You impressed me in that hallway, Homer. It's the least we can do, and if the song goes well, we'll stay in touch with each other."

"Yes, sir, that's fair enough," Homer said.

Homer walked onstage, playing a smooth groove to Catz's rhythm. Kiddy looked over at Pussley and nodded his head as they both smiled. It sounded good. Pussley started belting it out, Sum Tin had her backing vocals going well, and the drums were kicking it—the song was flying on its own. The sax fills in between allowed Homer to show his interpretation of the tune, and they fit very nicely. When the spotlight usually hit Catz for his solo, it came down on Homer instead. His solo was part Catz's and part Homer's, and this black cat really did shine. There was much appreciation from the crowd. When the song came to its completion, everyone stood and gave the band an ovation. Homer closed his eyes and bowed humbly, which caused the audience to cheer even more. He walked off the stage, waving.

Pussley, glimpsing her setlist, took off with the next song. Their show finished with Catz and Sum Tin's, "A Gift Divine," which left the audience purring and meowing happily, while they sang together. Tinkles even mused in his mind that these two could be their own act as a duo. It was that sweet sound of their vocals blending ...

Pussley came out at the end of their performance and told the audience that in a few minutes, "The best band in America would be out to entertain them."

But the instant feedback she was getting from everyone yelling back was that they were the best band! When Alex and the guitarist Tori from Kinfur heard that, their biggest fears were becoming a reality. In that crowd, they were becoming dethroned.

Tab heard it also and smiled because he believed in the Nine Lives' destiny. He knew they were going much higher up on the mountain than Kinfur had ever reached. Plus, Tab was also a business cat. He was very aware that because of Pussley Seasons and her band, all the shows would be sold out, and at this point in their careers, it had become all about the pay and the treats. They hadn't even introduced a new song for months, but the sudden change with Tabs's ongoing romance was causing emotions to stir, which for him would be a good time to put pencil to paper.

Pussley walked off and met everyone backstage. Max congratulated everyone, with a special thanks to Homer for bringing a new dynamic to the song that everyone enjoyed. Tinkles gave Homer his number and said to call him in a week so they could work something out. This made Homer smile from ear to ear, and he again thanked the band for allowing him to play.

Kiddy Rock said, "You did more than play, you created a new sound for the song. Heck, I'm all for you playing it again real soon."

He looked at Tinkles, who said, "Yeah, I was thinking the same thing."

Pussley agreed that the song sounded better with the sax.

Tinkles told Homer, "We're heading on to Detroit, and then we will end in Chicago. If you would like to play in those two cities with us, you are welcome."

In front of Homer, Tinkles asked Max, "Maxi, can we get him some pay for his part?"

"I don't see why not, Tinkles. It was a smooth sound and worth exploring."

This led Kiddie Rock to say, "I guess we'll see you in Detroit, cool cat."

"Indeed, you will." He smiled and bid them good night.

The next morning, room service was ordered, and they delivered a wonderful breakfast fare. The smell alone was waking everyone up.

Claire Dainty, while rubbing her eyes, told Maxi she had to get one of the security guards to stay with them because there was so much money changing hands so quickly. She also told Max, "The four thousand shirts you ordered were completely sold—every hoodie, cup, and keychain was also gone from the shelves.

"The security guard was so nice that he had called a partner who wheeled in a small but heavy safe for us to put all of the proceeds into."

When Claire handed Max the receipts for the total items sold, his eyes became as wide as a deer in the headlights.

That's when he decided that this was going to be a side business apart from the band, but still have a percentage going to the label. Those are details he would discuss with Hymee, his sister, and Felinia very soon.

This managing a rock band with shining stars was a lot of fun, Max thought.

"I've Got to Carry On"

I was born in a cold stone graveyard
Under a big ole shady tree
From there my mama would take us
To a porch that was fulla bees
We would walk a forever mile
And down to the river's edge
So's to wash us and a'clean us
And keep the bugs from our furry heads
I've got to carry on
I see no other way
I got my start a bit rough
But that'll be okay
I've got to carry on
It's like my momma always said
It's better living a life with pain
Than to struggle with your self-made chains

Chapter 32

While riding on the bus, Tinkles was sitting back and thinking: How wonderful that these really good songs are being created by us. It's like Kit, Catz, and I are tuned in to a special radio station that only we can hear—you're listening to KHIT, where the hits just keep on coming—and we are able to pair these lyrics with these beautiful melodies that just keep drifting into our minds! Tinkles wonders, are we being watched from above to see if we're going to give it away in the same way that it was given to us? The way it was placed in our paws so easily, the way our hearts received it? Maybe when we're connected more deeply, this heavenly station is turned on for us. We must have the ears to listen, the spirit to receive it, and the God-given talent for these songs to be played by us to flow over everyone listening. This is the way that it is supposed to happen, like an anointing. I suppose in some ways, it can parallel a Gospel choir full of praise.

Felinia, who is in the sedan with the other queens, is fast asleep and dreaming. She is wildly playing like a kitten with Kiddy Rock, tearing up a ball of yarn. But also, words are appearing to her, and within her dreaming mind, everything narrows to a page on the table in front of her. It's a blank page that she feels the need to fill, and in her dream this is what she writes:

I've got to go and find her
There is no other way
If I'm to have this closure
Leave my sorrow far away
I must be reunited
Let our joy embrace the day
That my mother, bless her heart
Gave me life and played her part
For which I praise her in every way
I've got to go and find her…find her
For there's no other way.

She awoke with the queens getting out of the sedan and strolling into the lobby of the hotel. She immediately ran to the front counter and grabbed a page of their stationery. Finding a pen, she wrote the words down. Later that afternoon, she and Kiddy Rock were talking, and she presented the lyrics from her dream to him to see what he thought of it.

He loved it! He also understood it, because he, too, was an orphan. He asked her, "May I add something to this?"

She replied, "That would make me very happy."

He said, "Okay then. I need complete silence to gather my thoughts. I will see you in a little while, after I come up with something."

She understood. Songwriters always have a myriad of ways to put their ideas down on the page.

This is what he wrote from his heart:

My search it will continue with patience and
    His Grace
My day-by-day reminder the next town may be
    the place
That I find her, and if and when I ever do
It will end with a long embrace
My tears will run all through my fur giving joy to
    my happiest face
Mother could you hear me on the nights I
    cried alone
When the tears from my misfortune fell like rain
    from up above
I know it wasn't your fault, for the timing was
    all wrong
To bring me into this mixed-up world where I truly
    didn't belong

Although there was something deep inside that he'd been living with for some time, Kiddy Rock was feeling rewarded—enjoying companionship, great music, and being part of a close family—all the things that he never had but longed for were now laid at his feet. For which he was indeed very thankful.

The band was playing at the Lions Roar Auditorium, a ten-thousand-seater that's been sold out for two weeks already.

Upon entering the hotel, one of the staff members mentioned that Ethereal Vibes would be down at the other end of the floor they were on. This was a band that Pussley grew up listening to and idolizing. She could sing many of their songs. Their extremely talented queen vocalist, Carmen Bleu, was someone she had always wanted to meet, and the very thought that it might happen was exhilarating.

She asked Max if that was possible.

Max said, "Let me see what I can do."

It would be a first for Max, arranging for established talent to meet with up-and-coming new talent. He hoped there wouldn't be any egos involved, just a mutual respect of talented queens.

So, Maxi put in a call to Hymee to see how he should go about arranging things. Hymee was pleased that Max came to him. He told Max of a time when Carmen recorded in their studio and had much success with her single "When I Pounce, You Bounce."

Max didn't recall that older R&B tune, but the very fact that Hymee knew her just might be the open door for Pussley's possible meeting.

"I'll get back with you in a little bit, Max," said Hymee.

"Sure thing … and thanks, Hymee," said Max.

"I'll be glad to help these youngsters, Max."

Hymee made one call and secured a meeting for the band with Ethereal Vibes this evening, backstage at their uptown show. He told Max that Carmen Bleu was looking forward to meeting Pussley Seasons.

When Max told Pussley this, it was the first time he had seen her get nervous, which he thought was very cute. This was not the ultra-hip, classy, and cute lead singer, but the little queen in a room growing up, listening to records, and dreaming-of-such-a-meeting kind of cute.

When Max asked the band if they'd like to attend tonight's show, they all said, "Yes!"

"And you got us backstage, Maxi?" Kiddy Rock asked.

"I did," said Max.

"As far as managers go, Maxi, you are about the most professional I have ever known."

Right then and there, the band agreed, and for the second time, they saw Maxi blush.

Chapter 33

The band arrived an hour before showtime, and security ushered them into the dressing room of Carmen Bleu. Thanks to Max and Felinia, Pussley gave a beautiful bouquet of roses to Carmen for their introduction. Each member of the Nine Lives Five was introduced to her as well. Clearly, Carmen was taken aback by the respect the band showed her.

"Thank you, dear ones," she said to them all. "You know I have heard you sing, and it is like hearing angels. I have also heard you, Pussley, singing as a vixen."

Everyone laughed.

"Oh, that's just my stage persona," Pussley said sheepishly. The audience expects what they perceive me to be, and I'm just up there trying to give them what they're hoping for.

"Well, that was a wise choice of words, dear," said Carmen. "Sounds like you've learned a lot in your short time with the Nine Lives Five."

"It's been a whirlwind every day!" Pussley said.

"I was there at one time, dear. I was there," Carmen said. "But now, these ongoing tours are for nostalgia, bringing back the wonderful memories so many of us felines have."

"Well, I'm definitely one of those," said Pussley, touching Carmen's paw with her own.

Tinkles asked if she still sang "A Moment in Time."

"I do!" she said, surprised. "You're familiar with that one? I've played it on the piano for years."

Pussley chimed in, saying, "I know that song well."

"You do? Just the other day, my manager and I were thinking about doing something different for my shows. So, I'll put this out there … what if your friend Tinkles here, and you and I sing it together? The piano and voices. I think that might be a nice treat for the audience."

Tinkles said, "I would be honored."

Pussley said, "I don't know what to say ... except thank you from the bottom of my heart for making another dream of mine come true. Life for me lately has been a fulfillment of dreams," she said with tears in her eyes. "And I am just so very grateful to the One above, who has made all of this possible."

"Dear kitten, there's not a day that goes by that I don't thank Him for my life and everything in it."

"Go ahead and get yourself to wardrobe. About halfway through the show, I'll let the audience know I have guests. It should be a lot of fun."

"The most!" said Pussley.

"Somebody pinch me," said Tinkles.

Carmen laughed.

Max and the band were given seats up front, where they were all giggling and having a great time being on the other side of the stage for a change, coming to see someone very talented, as they had done for so many years.

Tinkles was going over the song with Carmen's pianist, just so he and Carmen would be on the same page.

Carmen asked Pussley, "Who is that other young queen that sings with you?"

"Oh, you mean my backup vocalist, Sum Tin. Yes, she has a lovely voice, also."

"There's a uniqueness to you three that I've heard and am very fond of. Would you like to see if she knows the song, Pussley?"

"Sure, Carmen. I'll go ask her."

Pussley practically pounced down to the front of the stage, leaned over, and asked Sum Tin, "Are you familiar with the song, 'A Moment in Time'?"

"Oh yes!" she said. "I sang that song many times in the bath."

"Well, Carmen is asking if you would like to sing it with us?"

"Me? Sing with Carmen Bleu? That is very gracious of her," Sum Tin said.

"Well, come on back and we'll go through it once."

Tinkles was beside himself. He and Sum Tin were going to be up on the same stage singing with Carmen Bleu … a memory they would share forever!

Halfway through her wonderful show, Carmen introduced Pussley Seasons, Tinkles, and Sum Tin from the Pussley Seasons and the Nine Lives Five band.

The older cats were meowing and whistling, but the younger felines who knew her music well went cat crazy! This brought a big smile to Carmen's face. Carmen looked back at Tinkles and nodded her head for the cue. Carmen sang a verse by herself with Tinkles on piano, and it was as beautiful as always—then, the three of them joined her for the rest of the song. It was sheer magic. Everyone was mesmerized by such angelic voices singing with Carmen's.

Thank Goodness Carmen's sound techs were recording this for posterity, because this would make a new single for each of them. Carmen's recording would be in the R&B genre. Pussley's would have it as one of their sweet ballads, and they would also take it to the studio. They would see about adding some of the band's instrumentation, exploring the possibilities.

With her Ethereal Vibes show now over, she came backstage to speak with the reassembled Nine Lives band. Carmen had nothing but praise for meeting them all.

She said, "Singing with Pussley, Sum Tin, and Tinkles was a sheer joy. I mean no disrespect to my pianist, but Tinkles, I believe I liked your version better."

Tinkles just bowed his head and said, "Thank you so much for your kind words, Carmen."

As they were leaving, Carmen said to them, "Let's do this again, shall we?"

Max said, "I'll talk with Hymee, and we'll arrange it."

"Oh, my God! Hymee the Himalayan?" Carmen gushed. She said to Max, "Tell Hymee I said thank you for being instrumental in getting my career off the ground."

"I will do that, Carmen," said Max.

The band piled into the limo for the drive back to the hotel. All of them were chattering, meowing, and purring about how wonderful the evening had been. It was all because of their wonderful manager and friend ... Maxipuss Maxwell.

"A Moment in Time"

Our days they do run by so very, very fast
Seem always a blur, and never really last
A slow train that's coming, and never, ever stops
Still, I do appreciate all those days I've lived,
    riding to the top
A moment in time, when a pause comes my way
When I'm able to see how He lightens my day
He's been there forever, by my side I must say
And shows me His love that won't ever go away

Someone say "Amen."

Chapter 34

Pussley woke up, remembering the events of last night and smiling. The second thing on her mind was, why not have Carmen sing her song the way we did last night at the Ethereal Vibes show? After all, she did tell us that she was once there in front of large crowds, but she seemed sad when she mentioned it. So I will present her an opportunity to sing to a new and large audience again—an audience of ten thousand wailing felines and canines. That should surely boost her spirits!

She ran down the hall to Max's room, knocked on the door, and Claire opened it. She had arrived already, and they were engrossed in the scheduling of this evening's events.

"What's up, kitten?" Max asked.

"I would very much like to have Carmen sing at our show this evening with our new version of her song!"

"Wow! I think that's a wonderful idea, Pussley! I'll bet that she would absolutely love that," Max said. "I will personally go down to the front desk and find out what room she occupies, and we will go ask her together."

Pussley purred at that. Max told the two queens he would be right back, then went down to the front desk and told them the story about what took place last night with Carmen Bleu. He explained that they want to return the favor. The desk clerk made a call up to her room, and when Carmen sleepily answered, the clerk handed Max the phone.

He began with, "Carmen? This is Max, manager for the Nine Lives Five."

"Yes, Max. Good morning. How may I help you?"

"Pussley and I would like to come to your room and ask you a question. Would you entertain seeing us for a moment?"

"That would be fine. Give me an hour so that I can get ready."

"Of course, Carmen," said Max. "We do appreciate your time, and we'll see you a little later."

Max came back to the room and told Pussley, "We have an appointment with Carmen Bleu in an hour."

Pussley ran away giggling like a little school kitten.

Like Carmen, she also had to get ready. While she was sitting in front of the mirror, staring at herself, she just couldn't believe that she was becoming friends with Carmen Bleu, a beautiful and extremely talented queen whom she had admired for years.

In another part of the hotel, in front of another mirror, Carmen wonders what she will be asked by Pussley. *Probably something about our future records*, she supposes.

After an hour, there was a knock on Carmen's door. When she opened it, Pussley put her paws around her, kissed her cheek, and said, "I had the most wonderful time last night! I do hope you did also."

"Dear," Carmen began, "I haven't sung that song like that in many years. For the first time in a long time, I felt young again! So, I just want to say thank you, Pussley, for making that happen!"

"Well, Carmen, that's why we're here."

The two queens, still enthralled with their greeting, had totally forgotten that Max was standing behind them! He was silent and smiling at these two top-of-their-game queens.

"Oh my!" said Carmen, "Where are my manners! Hello, Max," Carmen said, walking up to him, embracing him, and kissing him on his cheek.

Max, now blushing, said, "This is a delight, seeing you again so soon, Carmen."

"Come in, come in. Let's sit out on the balcony under the umbrella."

As they were walking that way, a knock came on the door.

Carmen said, "Oh my! This is a busy morning!"

She went to the door, and it was the room service she had ordered. Lifting the tray's lid so that they could all see the edible delights, she asked, "I do hope you two have an appetite?"

Being the tom, Max said, "I can eat!"

Pussley looked at her and said, "I'll nibble."

"Good, good," Carmen said. "Let's fix a plate and go outside."

As they were enjoying their caviar and shrimp biscuits—with a special flavored cream that Carmen enjoys—Pussley looked at Carmen and asked, "Carmen, how would you like to sing the song that we performed at your show last night, at our show tonight? It'll be at the Lions Roar Auditorium. Ten thousand sold-out seats filled with adoring fans will be able to hear the same magic that we heard last night!

Carmen stared at Pussley with a blank face. The gravity of this question was slowly sinking in, turning her face into the biggest smiling kitty face they had ever seen. This now had everyone smiling!

"Oh my, Pussley!" she gasped! "Now you honor me. I can't think of a more lovely way to spend an evening than to sing our version at your show. And here I thought I was going to stay in for the evening." Meowing loudly, she asked Pussley, "Come here, dear, and give Carmen a hug."

Pussley practically jumped into her lap, and the two queens, weeping between smiles, made Max believe he was in the right business.

Max told her, "I'll work out the details. Pussley will come tell you when to arrive and where to meet the two security guards who will usher you to the dressing rooms. This is going to be a fun night ... I can feel it," said Max.

"Indeed, it is!" said Carmen.

"I'm so glad you said yes!" Pussley gushed.

Before leaving, Pussley turned to Carmen and said, "You know, I believe we're going to have our own hits from this!"

"Oh, I am so tickled thinking about it!" said Carmen. "Thank you so very much for thinking of me."

"It's all I've been doing all night," Pussley said, smiling. "See you in a little while, Carmen."

"Goodbye, dear."

"We'll see you this evening," said Max.

Pussley couldn't wait to tell Tab of the good fortune they've had and how tonight he'll get to hear them singing one of Carmen Bleu's standards, "A Moment in Time."

Tab said, "I know that one. I used to sing that before I got into Kinfur. How did you make this happen?"

Pussley told him the whole story, and he just smiled quietly, listening to all of her words. Then he said, "Pussley, I couldn't be happier for you. You are living the life I hoped you would be, and I can honestly say your star will shine for years to come."

With that, she wrapped her paws around his neck and kissed him long and sweet. Upon stopping, she looked into his eyes and said, "I am so falling for you, Tab."

"Kitten, I'm already there, and I'll open my paws to catch you."

Hearing that, she gave him another kiss and said, "I've got to run and tell the others about the epic night we're going to have."

Tab said, "Shout it from the rooftops, Kitten! Now you're starting to enjoy the perks of rock stardom."

Stopping at the door, Pussley said, "Tab, that is the first time anyone has referred to me as being a rock star." She meowed, then walked away purring.

Tab just smiled, watching her leave.

The Nine Lives Five sound check was at 2:00 p.m. There was no need to have Carmen there. She was a consummate professional, a seasoned vocalist who knew her way around a song.

The band sounded wonderful playing three numbers, very tight. They were now ready for this evening's Detroit performance. Before leaving, the band was told by Pussley that Carmen would be a guest this evening to sing her song the way they did last night.

Catz said, "Oh, you're going to kill it tonight!"

Kiddy Rock said, "If you're half as good as you were last night, this place will see cool cat chaos in all of its forms."

The band smiled, knowing full-well that being seen with Carmen on stage raised the bar, their credibility, and most of all their cat-crazy appeal—not to mention it meant a very possible number one hit for all of them!

This has been the best roller coaster ride ever!

Chapter 35

With the success of the Detroit show, several members of Kinfur are acting out their kitten-like emotions. Jealousy is at the top of the list—towards Pussley Seasons and the Nine Lives Five. They are trying to spread rumors of improprieties; accusations of stealing ticket sales money; throwing wild parties—anything to bring the Nine Lives' train to a halt. This has Max and the band hurt and angered by the lies being spread about them, something they had been shielded from until now. They had been unaware of the repercussions from such falsehoods.

However, Philly is aware that it all started with Alex and Tori. He, Tab, and Cornwallis know what has to be done. For these two oblivious and malevolent toms, Chicago will be their last show.

Hymee and the label execs went to bat for the Nine Lives band to offset any potential fallout that may hurt the band and their record sales. They put together an interview article with those who know them personally, speaking honestly and candidly about how good and down-to-earth the cats of this band really are—and also to vilify the media's inept handling of the shameful and alleged gossip without an ounce of verification. It will come out in next month's issue of Bounce and Role, and thankfully, it will appear after their Chicago performance.

The band's manager, Philly Shnizlestix, will issue a statement about Alex's and Tori's sudden departure from Kinfur "due to creative differences."

Karma never forgets … and neither does Philly.

Arriving in the Windy City, the band has been practically demanding to get several deep dish pizzas to the hotel forthwith, or there will be an all-out dietary mutiny with every cat for themselves. The queens would still like to try some of what Pussley had described eating in Carmen's room the other day. Those caviar with shrimp biscuits sounded so yummy to them.

The yelling, screaming, and caterwauling coming from down the hall in Kinfur's rooms had hotel security banging on their doors. They were telling them to bring it down to a dull roar or they would have to leave … an awkward state of affairs for Kinfur.

Pussley called Tab and asked if he would like to go for a stroll on the Chicago Riverwalk. Tab replied, "You read my mind, kitten. I'll meet you down in the lobby in ten."

Kiddy Rock and Felinia are already there, talking future plans of creating a family where all the kittens are adopted and given a life of love and happiness … something they never got the chance to have till now.

Tinkles and Sum Tin are playing with their harmonies for tomorrow night's show with Carmen Bleu, along with a few other melodies that Tinkles has been working on. Tinkles is giving her the direction for what he's hearing in his mind.

Max and Claire Dainty are working on the schedule for tomorrow, trying to make sure that everything will run smoothly.

Philly calls Max and lets him know that Alex and Tori will no longer be with Kinfur after tomorrow night and asks if he happens to know any bassists or guitarists talented enough to audition for the band while on hiatus.

"I know several, Philly. Following tomorrow's show, I will reach out and make some calls."

"That would be great, Max. I would owe you big time."

"You won't owe me a thing, Philly. The way you came to my aid to save Felinia has me owing you. You still have your moxie, and I admire that. We'll find you a few talented toms."

"All right then, biker dude, I'll see you tomorrow evening."

"Indeed, you will, Tabby One."

Chapter 36

The anticipation backstage can be cut with a knife. Everyone is coming out of wardrobe, and their makeup looks so current, so professional. PQ has always been on top of it, making sure this band looks as sharp as possible. They have every crease pressed, every cuff and collar starched, all shoes polished till they glisten, and Yanx doesn't even look out of place with his custom sleeveless band attire. Rather, he is the epitome of what a rock drummer can and should look like, who is playing in a tight, hit-making, touring rock band that is working tirelessly night after night, city after city, stage after stage. For sheer percussive wizardry, they don't get any better than Yanx the Manx.

Pussley and Sum Tin look gorgeous in their rocked-out outfits. Pussley is wearing tight gray spandex tucked into her black boots, her white button-down shirt with oversized cuffs, and a matching gray vest with only the bottom buttoned. The light red scarf that she has worn since the very first show completes her Gypsy rock star persona.

Sum Tin is dressed in the same apparel as Pussley, but in the exact opposite colors, and this makes for a stunning contrast on stage. This is PQ's genius, and everyone loves it. Many a tomcat wishes they had the opportunity to date these two beautiful furry queens tonight, but they'll have to settle for a great rock show. Between the Nine Lives Five and Kinfur, it will be delivered.

Carmen Bleu is escorted to where the band is now standing, looking as elegant as ever in a long, tight-fitting, burgundy-sequined dress. Also, adorning her paws and neckline this evening are diamonds and rubies. She is the stunning example of what a classy and vivacious vocalist who has been fronting a top-tier R&B band for the past three decades looks like. She is given more respect than anyone on the stage this evening. She humbly approaches and greets the band members, who are taken aback by her poise and beauty. She saves a hug and a kiss for Max, who loves every moment of this.

Tab, Cornwallis, and Philly come up to greet the Nine Lives Five and their beautiful guest, with Philly gently taking Carmen's paw and kissing the top of it as he greets her.

This causes her to say, "Oh my!"

He introduces Tab and Cornwallis to her and adds, "We are thrilled to have you here with us this evening, Miss Bleu."

"Call me Carmen, please," she says.

Philly says, "As you wish. We can't remember when we were graced with vocal royalty such as yours, Carmen."

"Oh, you're good, Philly. A real smoothie," she says, smiling.

Everyone is smiling and preparing to take their places. Max has had a beautiful plush chair from the hotel sent for Carmen to relax in until her performance, and it will stay with her all through their show.

While Claire Dainty handles any and all questions, Tinkles finally gets to see her. He comes and gives her a beautiful hug and kiss, telling her, "I adore you." This melts her heart and causes her to weep while she watches him take the stage.

Catz walks over to Sum Tin, and kisses her gently while saying in German, "Du siehst ehute abend so hubsch aus." When she looks at him, puzzled, he says, "You look so lovely this evening." She then turns and floats to her place on stage.

Tab gives Pussley a very tender kiss and says, "This is your evening. You made this happen. Everyone here adores you, especially me. Have a most wonderful night, kitten. We'll talk again later," he says, as she goes to take her place.

Felinia is holding Kiddy Rock's paw and tells him, "I love being with a hero."

He bends down slightly, still holding her paw, and kisses her, then says, "I will be thinking of you the whole evening, waiting patiently to hold you in my paws."

"And that you shall have tonight, my knight." Both began laughing, and Kiddy Rock went to take his place.

The house lights go down, and for a moment, everything is quiet. The stage manager off to the side speaks into his radio, "Three … two … one … lights!"

With that, the tour de force begins! The audience is so excited and loud that if it weren't for the stage monitors, the band wouldn't be able to hear themselves play.

One after another, the Nine Lives Five perform their well-crafted songs, and thousands of fans sing along with them.

Carmen gets up from her chair, peeks out from behind the stage, and is floored by the sight. She has never sung to a crowd this excited and boisterous! Well … she was looking for something different for her show, and if there was ever something different … this is it! Carmen, for a moment, actually felt butterflies in her tummy. This caused her to pause and say, "Oh my!" Nonetheless, she stood there, grateful for these wonderful young felines wanting her to be a part of their world.

She now hears Pussley introducing her, "Tonight you are all in for a real treat. We have been blessed with a guest who has great talent for a song. This lovely queen is always seen singing on stage, where she can do no wrong. Let's give a huge, warm Chicago welcome to my friend, the classy and ethereal Miss Carmen Bleu."

With that, a thunderous applause erupts! Carmen has never experienced anything like this!

As she gracefully walks out, she and Pussley meet in the middle and give each other a heartfelt hug. Sum Tin walks over, and they stand under the boom mic that has been lowered for them. The applause dies down, and Tinkles begins the beautiful melody by himself on his piano. Carmen begins singing the first verse, and it fills the arena. All eyes are upon her, stunned by her beauty and her passionate way of singing. Then Pussley, Sum Tin, and Tinkles come in with their harmonies. Many cats start crying, and many in the audience can be heard saying, "It sounds like angels singing!"

For a brief moment upon that stage, they have made those who are looking down from Heaven smile.

The magnitude of the decibel rating that came from the arena at the end of that song bordered on frightening. It could be heard several miles away!

Pussley and Carmen hugged once again. Carmen walked off the stage while waving goodbye, and Pussley watched her go. Carmen met Max on the other side of the curtain, where he threw his paws around her and kissed her on her lips! He then looked at her, saying, "That was the most beautiful rendition of your song I have ever heard sung."

Pussley looked back into the wide expanse of fans and asked, "What do you think of the voice of Carmen Bleu?"

Once again, there was pandemonium in the audience with wailing, screeching, barking, and roaring—every sound that dogs and cats can create with their throats was heard.

Max, looking at Carmen as they listened to the crowd's applause, said, "That's all for you, dear. They love you. Heck, I love you!" Max said, without fear or hesitation.

Carmen looked at him, took a step forward, and kissed him. Then she said, "I could fall for someone like you."

"And I'd like to be there when you do," said Max.

They both laughed, knowing that they would somehow start seeing each other.

Pussley Seasons was called back onstage for an encore. She then waved goodbye, saying, "Kinfur will be out in a moment to rock your world!" More wonderful applause!

The band agreed this was the most appreciative crowd they had ever played for. Kinfur and Philly came and congratulated them on a fantastic show and showered praise on Carmen for her performance.

Philly said, "Carmen, we have a European tour beginning next month. I believe I speak for everyone here when I say we would like to see you in some of those cities singing with the Nine Lives Five. Is that something you might entertain?"

Max looked at her and said, "How about it, Carmen?"

Every cat present is now waiting for her response.

"Yes! Most definitely yes! You flatter me!"

As she grabbed Max's paw, everyone present came in for a huge group hug and thanked each other for one great big, beautiful evening.

Chapter 37

Pussley and her band were flown back to Purrville, rested and refreshed, with plenty of new material to take into the studio to create their second album.

But first things first. Maxi took some time to make good on his promise to Philly. He called several guitarists and bassists from his past who were of the caliber Philly needed to fill the void created by Kinfur's losses. He hoped they would serve Kinfur well on their up-and-coming European tour.

The studio was booked for the following week. This downtime would give the band the R&R they needed and were looking for. Those who found a mate on their journey now had a little time to indulge in their feelings and desires openly, developing the bonds that would carry them through the next chapter of their lives.

Europe was around the corner and would be another learning experience to create songs from. There would be different cultures and new adventures…all the things young musicians dream and write about. Their time back in Purrville was a new type of culture shock. Wherever any of them were seen, they were congratulated, asked for their autographs, or begged to have pictures taken with fans. It would seem they had become the property of Purrville! Privacy seemed to be a thing of the past. Anonymity no longer applied to their lives. They were bona fide rock stars who happened to live in Purrville, and this would take some getting used to.

For the time being, Pussley could only talk to Tab by phone. They had not yet figured out the logistics of a long-distance romance, but their willingness to go the full mile would give them the fuel to see it through.

Kiddie Rock and Felinia were not wasting any time either. They were already inquiring into the adoption agencies available and the processes necessary to fulfill their dreams. They were also trying to decide whose house they would live in and whose would be sold.

Tinkles and Claire Dainty went and stayed for the week in a bed and breakfast. They spent all their time together, having great conversations about their future, taking long walks through the nearby park, and discussing what Europe is going to be like. But the most fun of all was just being a couple.

Catz and Sum Tin spent their time on a six-day cruise in the northern Atlantic. Traveling on the ship allowed them to become tightly knit, something they both enjoyed immensely. During the cruise, they enjoyed delicious meals, hours of talking in the open air, looking into the sea, watching the whales play, and making plans for their future. Something that was also very important to them was perfecting their harmonies together, which were very powerful, melodic, and natural. This practice would lend itself greatly to their band's studio sessions.

Yanx was still single, and he wanted it that way. He took a leisurely drive down to Nashville to take in the local music scene, a drum seminar by a jazz drummer that he idolized, and he participated in several sit ins with some of the more contemporary acts that were playing. He picked up the drum set he'd had his eye on for some time, straight from the factory. He was given a bonus tour of their facility in appreciation for not only his desire to own one, but for his endorsement of it as well. Photos were taken, and the acknowledgment of his peers within the industry was satisfying enough, but having them ask for his autograph along with their pictures taken together was icing on the cake.

Hymee the Himalayan spent the week preparing for the Nine Lives Five's next album. A lot would be riding on it, and he wanted nothing left to chance because, as he put it, their success is the label's success also. All videos that had been taken of their shows would be watched by all of them. They would comment on select pieces for promotional marketing and choose which live-action videos would be released to fulfill the desire of their fans to hear and see new things coming from them. It would be an interesting time for them. Hymee and the label execs were eager to be part of the dynamics of everyone working together.

And Max. Max was invited to Carmen's house on the coast, where they played house for the week, bouncing and roaring in their daily bliss, and where the topic of music never came up.

List of characters in the book:

Mushkins (Original Lead Singer)

Maxipuss Maxwell (Manager)

Pussley Seasons (Lead Singer)

Felix (PQ short for Prides Quarterly) (Wardrobe)

Claire Dainty (Max's Sister and Assistant)

Cutie Patootie (Makeup)

Pudee Wood (Owner of Club Pounce)

Kinfur (Touring Band)

Kitty Littré (Manager of the Nine Lives Five Fan Club)

Yanx the Manx (Drummer)

Sum Tin Wong (Siamese back-up vocalist for Pussley)

Catzenjammer (Catz) (Guitars) (Back-up Vocals)

Kiddy Rock (Bass)

Felinia (Band Runner and Vocalist)

Tinkles (Piano, Keyboard, and Vocals)

Philly Shnizlestix (Manager for Kinfur)

Muffins (Tab's Sister)

Puddin Cup (Graphic Artist)

Tab the Hunter (Lead Singer for Kinfur)

Cornwallis (Kinfur's Drummer and Philly's Nephew)

Hymee the Himalayan (CEO for Kitty Corner Records)

Kit Seasons (Pussley's Brother and Band Lyricist)

Homer Randolph (Saxophonist)

Tori (Guitarist for Kinfur)

Alex (Bassist for Kinfur)

Carlo Gaga (Philly's Half-brother/Limo Driver for Kitty
    Corner Records)

Vinny and Bobby Boombots (Philly's uncles)

Carmen Bleu (Lead Singer for Ethereal Vibes)